# My Dearest Waverley

## Cowboy Crossing
## Book 5

### Jessie Gussman

# Contents

# Acknowledgments

**Cover art by Julia Gussman**
**Editing by Heather Hayden**
**Narration by Jay Dyess**
**Author Services by CE Author Assistant**

———

Listen to the unabridged audio for FREE performed by Jay Dyess on the Say with Jay channel on YouTube. Get early access to all of Jay's recordings and listen to Jessie's books before they're available to the general public, plus get daily Bible readings by Jay and bonus scenes by becoming a Say with Jay channel member.

# Chapter One

"Daddy, I have to pee."

The little-girl voice came from the middle of the back seat of Zane Hudson's pickup as he drove south on Interstate 66 toward his hometown of Cowboy Crossing, Missouri.

He'd driven this road a million times, and even as he calculated in his head where the closest rest area or truck stop was, he looked in the rearview mirror at his sweet little daughter, Ophelia, tucked in a booster seat.

Her innocent blue eyes were scrunched, and her nose wrinkled. Zane was still on his first week of being a single dad to all four of his daughters, but already he knew that look wasn't one that would stand the test of the nickname of his state.

He didn't need his daughter to "show me" that she really had to go.

"Just wait five minutes," he said. His foot pressed harder on the accelerator. He typically tried to follow the speed limit—a law was a law—but this, quite frankly, seemed to constitute an emergency. "There's a truck stop right up ahead."

It was the worst truck stop in the state. The worst that he knew of, anyway, and he'd been all over, picking up cattle and equipment and delivering the same.

Still, it only took one more glance in the rearview mirror to give him the impression that his daughter's back teeth were floating. He needed to stop, and fast.

If he hadn't already come to that conclusion, his oldest daughter, Cordelia, who was sitting in the front seat beside him, turned her head and looked at him with worried eyes and pursed lips.

"Daddy? I think she really has to go. She can't ever wait."

"Well, she's just gonna have to until we get to the truck stop. I can't hardly stop along the road." His words were a little rough, but he tried to modulate his tone. He wasn't used to hanging around girls. After five years of constant struggling and court appearances and lawyers' fees and mediation meetings, he'd finally gotten custody of his girls.

Now he just had to learn how to be a dad.

He hadn't done a very good job of making his tone or his words female-approved, because Cordelia bit her lip, and her face fell before she turned and stared back out the windshield.

"I'm sorry." What should he have said? He didn't know. How did one talk to a little girl? Although Cordelia, at twelve, wasn't exactly a little girl. Not anymore. And he'd missed so much of her life.

She lifted a shoulder, not looking at him. "It's okay."

She spoke in a tone that communicated clearly that it was anything but okay, and he didn't know what to do about that, either.

He spoke in the sweetest, gentlest voice he could muster as he looked in the mirror at his youngest daughter. "Ophelia, can you please wait?"

His eyes shot back to the road, not wanting to wreck. He just caught the sign—two miles to the exit. His truck was already doing as much as it could, which was more than it should with the trailer hooked to the back.

Glad he'd only brought two of his four daughters, he gripped the wheel tightly as his heart thumped fast and hard in his chest. Who would've thought a little girl in the backseat could make his palms sweat and his neck throb?

But they were.

What was the worst thing that could happen?

A family mediator, one of several that his wife and he had dealt with in the early days before their divorce, had often asked that question.

At the time, Zane had pretty much rolled his eyes. He never understood the point of the question in his situation. The worst thing that could happen was that he could lose his girls.

But in other situations of life, it was a good question.

Take now. The worst thing that could happen was that she would pee in his truck, and it would smell like pee for the next twenty years. He certainly wasn't going to be able to afford a new truck before then at least.

Not with four daughters to raise.

His mother had already informed him when he dropped off his two middle children, Juliet and Beatrice, at her house this afternoon, unsure he could handle four kids and the bull he'd sold to a ranch just south of Jefferson City, that their clothes were too tight, too short, and generally too small. A shopping trip was in his future. He did not look forward to that.

His mother had offered to take them. Half-heartedly, because she didn't enjoy shopping, either.

But he was the dad. He'd fought long and hard for this privilege. He wasn't going to drop them off on his mother. So he would be going shopping. For clothes. Girls' clothes.

Where did a person buy girls' clothes?

He tried to remember if there'd been anything girl-like in the feed store where he usually bought his own stuff. Probably.

Maybe everything was unisex. He'd never even really paid attention. He just got stuff that fit and would wear well all day, boots being the most important part of his outfit.

Except in the winter, where a coat and gloves could make or break his day.

He highly suspected his knowledge of the apparel of the female species was going to be greatly multiplied in the coming weeks.

He welcomed it, even as he dreaded it.

"I want to be a good dad, Cordelia. I just need a little bit more practice." He said that low while looking out the windshield. It made him uncomfortable to admit weakness. As the oldest of six brothers, he'd been the leader. The one in charge. The one shouting orders and kicking the stragglers in the seat of their pants as they all followed their dad over the farm during his growing-up years.

His mother had been the sole spot of softness in their family.

It had been rough-and-tumble fun.

But it hadn't really prepared him for this.

Another shoulder shrug, and her arms crossed over her chest. "Whatever."

He suspected his ex, Vicki, had probably filled her head with horror stories of him from before their divorce.

There wasn't much he could do about it now.

She'd ended up with sole custody, and he'd had to fight for every visit he'd gotten, while she complained about everything he did, constantly going to her lawyer and taking him to court to try to keep him from seeing their girls.

She said he worked too much. Once, he'd walked out of the house and gone to the barn to feed the animals and left the girls sleeping in their beds. That one had kept him from seeing his girls for almost eighteen months. She'd convinced a judge he'd been neglectful. Supervised visits only. At her place which was an apartment in the suburbs of Cincinnati. He'd gone twice, and both times, he had felt like a criminal.

It'd been worth it to see his daughters, but he wouldn't wish the experience on anyone.

"Daddy, hurry." His daughter's voice sounded pinched and painful.

Thankfully, he had reached the lane for the exit and put his right turn signal on.

"We're stopping right now, sweetie. Just a couple more minutes."

He almost looked over at Cordelia, just to see if he'd done better that time, but he didn't. He couldn't live for her approval. He wasn't going to be a woman. As much as she might want him to be just like her mom, he wasn't ever going to be a mom. He wasn't even going to try. He did, however, want to be the best dad he could.

Maybe he was shortchanging his children by taking their mom out of their lives, but after she had dropped them off in an abandoned field outside of town and left them because she'd gone off her meds, it was definitely the best thing for them all.

Even the judge had come around to that conclusion.

Unfortunately, he wasn't going to be able to handle all four girls and still farm. He needed a housekeeper or a nanny or someone.

Someone good—excellent—but also cheap. His farm had been profitable for several years now, but he'd just dumped most of his available cash into buying his neighbor's spread—five hundred acres with road frontage and a store that had been used to sell fruit and produce.

If he'd known he was so close to getting his daughters...he probably would have still bought the land. It bordered his own property, and he couldn't pass it up.

It did leave him cash poor, though.

Stopping at the light, he took the right, then a quick left into the truck stop.

He'd stopped here twice before, which was two times too many in his opinion. It was the seediest, dirtiest, worst truck stop he'd ever been in in all of his travels.

It had been years since he'd stopped though, so maybe things had gotten cleaned out. Maybe it was under new management. Maybe there wasn't garbage all over the place and rough-looking guys hanging out near the weeds in the back lot, talking with just as rough-looking women.

Talking probably wasn't all they were doing. Not that he ever went back and checked. The first time he'd stopped, it had been because he had his youngest brother along and he'd had to use the restroom. The second time, he'd had to change a tire.

He certainly wouldn't have stopped for any other reason after the first time. He'd never expected to go back.

But this was an emergency. In the back, Ophelia was whimpering.

"Just a couple more minutes, baby. Hang on."

"She's not a baby. She's five." Cordelia lifted her brows and pursed her lips at him from the seat beside him.

If she had been raised with him, she would never have been allowed to get away with that attitude. But this was their first week in his home, and he didn't want to have that fight.

He probably would never get her to respect him the way he wanted her to, not with her background and the things she'd probably been told about him. The majority of which would be untrue, although Vicki could tell some stories that would make him look really bad, and they would be mostly true.

He hadn't been a perfect angel all his life.

He'd never cheated on her.

That was more than she could say.

She had flaunted it.

Cordelia probably didn't know, but Vicki had been pregnant with Cordelia when they'd gotten married.

She wasn't his, though he'd always accepted her like she was, and his name was on her birth certificate.

He highly doubted Vicki had told her that.

Perhaps she'd figured it out herself. Since Vicki had blue eyes, and so did he, it was physically impossible for them to have a brown-eyed baby.

Cordelia's eyes were brown.

Her hair was also tightly curled and almost black versus the golden-brown color of the rest of the girls' straight hair.

Maybe she'd noticed a difference, and that was part of her attitude.

He didn't know. He wasn't a psychologist. Although, he'd been to so many counselors over the years, just trying to do whatever it took to be able to at least see his girls, he could speak the language a little. Not that he wanted to. All he ever wanted to do was farm and raise a family.

Because he was pulling a trailer, he pulled into the big truck section of the lot and came to a stop. They always put the trucks further away from the building, which made sense, since they were bigger and took more space.

It stunk now though, because he had to get his daughter across the big lot and into the building and then find the right bathroom.

Thankfully, this truck stop didn't have all the steps that some of them did, the ones where they were sitting kind of up on a hill. This one was flat to the ground, so no one hundred steps to navigate before he got his daughter to the bathroom.

He froze in the act of opening his car door.

How was he going to get her into the bathroom?

His eyes slid over to Cordelia. "Do you have to go too?"

"Yeah." She didn't look at him as she jerked her door open.

His relationship with her wasn't exactly one where he could ask her to take her little sister and go to the bathroom. Commanding her to do it would be more like him anyway.

But he'd just gotten custody. Did he want Cordelia going to the judge and saying he abandoned them at this dirty truck stop? Broken glass crackled as his boot came out of the truck and landed on the ground.

He slammed the door shut and opened the back door to let Ophelia out.

Glancing around the parking lot, he calculated that it was only about half full. What were the odds that the men's restroom would be empty?

Could he somehow scope it out and then stand guard at the door while his daughters went in there?

Maybe if this were a normal stop, he could do that. But he could hardly think that Ophelia could wait while the restroom emptied out.

He absolutely couldn't let them go anywhere by themselves out of his eyesight. Not in this dump. What was he going to do?

# Chapter Two

Waverley Madris hunched her shoulder, trying to keep her purse on it, as she held tight to the hands of her two youngest sons, Roman, who was five, and Ax, who was six.

She had never stopped at this truck stop before. She had hoped she had enough gas to make it to where she was meeting August Stetto to deliver the baked goods she'd made for his craft fair, but her car was saying five miles to empty and she still had twenty miles to go. She needed to put her last five bucks in the gas tank and hope August paid her cash, so she could get home.

If Waverley had known what terrible shape the truck stop was in...she would have stopped anyway.

She'd made the boys wait to use the restroom until she'd paid for and pumped her gas.

She should have refused to deliver the goods.

That wasn't true. She would never have refused work. She needed every cent she could get, although there was no way, barring a miracle, she was going to make rent this month. She hadn't even paid for last month's rent.

She'd had the money, but before she'd taken it to her landlord, her oven had quit. She paid a repairman fifty bucks to come out and tell her it wasn't repairable, and then she'd had to choose between paying rent or having a working oven which she needed in order to make the baked goods that she and her children depended on selling in order to survive.

She'd chosen the oven and gone to see her landlord, explaining the problem.

He'd been very understanding, and had not made her pay the rent, but had simply asked her to try to get it to him as soon as she could.

And she'd had it, all except for fifty dollars, when her third son, Luke, who was not currently with her since he and her two oldest boys had stayed home to help Deacon Hudson dig up the church's backed-up septic system, had stepped on a nail.

It wasn't the first son she'd had that had stepped on a nail, but it was the first son she'd had that had stepped on a nail pushing it in to the point where she couldn't pull the nail out. She'd had to take him to the emergency room, where they charged her five hundred and forty-nine dollars for the privilege of removing said nail.

If she'd had his older brother hold 'im and then pulled as hard as she could, she probably could have gotten the nail out. But even though she hadn't been able to pay the rent, again, the five hundred and forty-nine dollars had been well spent, since the emergency room had morphine, and she did not.

"John," she said, speaking to her fourth son, "stay close to me." How many times in her life had she wished for more than two hands? This was another one of those times.

John might be eight and more than capable of handling himself, but she didn't like the looks of this place. She wouldn't let him out of her sight.

"Yes ma'am," John said seriously. Too seriously for an eight-year-old. But there wasn't anything she could do about it right now. Maybe ever.

Things had been bad when her husband was alive. He wasn't kind, putting it mildly, although he had never hit her or their children. Maybe she should have left him. There were lots of people who would say she was a fool for staying. But when she gave her word, it meant something to her.

She just wished she hadn't been so quick to pledge her life to a man who turned out to be rotten.

A memory flashed through her mind, but she pushed it aside. She'd married the man her parents had wanted her to, but not until she'd asked the man she'd actually wanted to marry, first.

He'd declined.

She considered her husband's death almost a gift from God, if such a thing could be true. Almost like Abigail and Nabal in the Bible.

After a year of struggling to make it on her own, she wasn't certain if it was a gift—not anymore. He might not have been a nice man, but at least he'd brought home a paycheck. They'd never been evicted.

She had a feeling that was about to change.

John took both hands and pulled on the door to the convenience store. Duct tape followed a crack in the glass diagonally down the top part of the door.

Leaning back, John put all of his weight into it, and the door opened grudgingly.

Waverley waited, clutching the hands of Ax and Roman. Normally Roman talked a mile a minute, and it was hard for anyone else in the family to get a word in edgewise. But even he seemed cowed by the foreboding atmosphere of the truck stop.

It almost felt like it could be something out of a horror movie. There had been grass growing up in the cracks of the sidewalk, and three of the four gas pumps were out of order. Thankfully, there hadn't been a line.

Roman had needed to come in and use the restroom. She couldn't send him in by himself, not with the way that place looked, and she wasn't going to leave the other two boys out in the car, no matter how self-reliant they seemed to be for their age. She just wasn't taking that risk. This seemed like the kind of place where children were abducted and sold, never to be seen again.

Maybe the state would eventually come and take her children if she couldn't support them, but she wasn't going to lose them to an unknown, unnamed, and uninvited party.

She might be poor, but that didn't mean she loved her children any less than someone with more money.

There were a lot of times she wished she could go back and make different choices, but she tried not to waste too much time living in the past. As bleak as the future looked.

She shook all of that out of her head and walked in the door.

"Thank you, John," she said, walking through then slowing as John walked in and the door creaked shut slowly behind him.

They'd stepped right into the convenience store part of the big building, although half of the shelves were empty.

A sour-looking man in his thirties or forties sat behind the counter, glaring at her like he was afraid she or her children were going to shoplift something. She felt like holding her hands up in innocence, but that would mean letting go of her boys, and there was no force on earth that could make her do that right now.

Sweeping her eyes around the store, she saw an arrow and a yellow sign that said "restrooms."

"This way, boys." She marched forward with determination. This shouldn't take long. That was one advantage boys had over girls. They might be messier, and she might've spent more time than she ever thought she would teaching the six of them how to "aim." A skill her teenage self would never have dreamed that anyone would need to possess to control the liquids that came out of their body, let alone teach to someone else. Not that she possessed it, she'd just taught it, to all six of her boys. Some more successfully than others.

At any rate, she didn't even care about aim right now. All she really cared about was getting done what they needed to do and getting out of here. This place gave her the creeps.

That was saying something. She'd suffered through a horrendous marriage and was raising six boys alone. There wasn't too much that could ruffle her.

"John, you're going in the ladies' restroom with me and Ax and Roman."

"Aw, Mom."

Just two words, but she wouldn't even allow that under normal circumstances. However, she let his disrespect slide for now, because she wasn't going to make a scene. Not here of all places.

"Wrong answer," she said instead, calmly, her voice carrying none of the anxiety that whipped around in her stomach. She'd long ago learned that her children looked to her for emotional cues. When they fell down, if she was smiling when they looked up, they had more of a tendency to laugh instead of cry.

She'd smiled through an awful lot of hard stuff.

But even she couldn't dredge up a smile for this place. She knew her face had her serious look on, and she didn't even try to modulate it with any relaxing of her lips.

"Yes ma'am," John said, his tone correct but his body language still signaling that he thought he was way too mature to be walking into the ladies' restroom.

Under normal circumstances, Waverley would agree. But it was better for her eight-year-old to possibly make a few ladies in the ladies' restroom uncomfortable than for him to be in the men's restroom alone.

"You can go in first, then wait for me." She gave instructions as they finished walking down the hall and turned left, the ladies' restroom door coming into view. "Do not under any circumstances leave this bathroom without me."

The boys chorused yes ma'ams together, then Waverley let go of Ax and pulled on the door. It was just as stiff as the front door.

Letting go of Roman's hand, she put both hands on the handle and pulled with all her might. It moved but didn't quite open.

She had never been in a public restroom where the door had been stuck so tightly.

Making a mental note to never, ever stop at this truck stop again, she braced her feet on the floor, hands on the handle, and yanked with all her might.

The door stuck, then let loose abruptly, and she stumbled back, smacking into the back wall. Her boys smiled as they trooped into the bathroom.

Waverley had to grin too. She probably looked like an idiot. Like she was having a fight with the door, which she kind of was.

But she'd won, so there was that.

Taking a deep breath and ignoring the cracked plaster and the overhead light that blinked with a dim weariness that was the exact opposite of the tenacity the door had displayed in clinging to the frame, Waverley walked in, pushing against the door which wanted to slam shut behind her.

How did little old ladies go to the restroom in this place? If she had been any weaker, she wouldn't have gotten the thing open.

She turned the corner and skidded to a stop as her eyes met those of a...man.

She'd just fought the door. She'd seen the picture of the person wearing a skirt on the other side of it—had been face-to-face with a placard that said "woman."

She was in the right place.

Her kids wouldn't have let her go anywhere else, if there had been any doubt.

She felt her cheeks heat. The man didn't look like a serial killer, although she'd heard serial killers could be good-looking, as this man was.

But something about the open honesty on his face calmed her, or maybe it was his cowboy hat and the work boots on his feet. He was just a good old boy in the wrong spot.

She'd actually been in a men's restroom several times. Something about being nine months pregnant and having her full bladder being squashed like a pancake on her pelvic floor made her not care what bathroom was open. She'd rushed in at least twice to the wrong spot and not realized she was in the wrong place until she was no longer in intense pain. Of course, by then it was far too late to save her dignity.

So she knew that men's restrooms didn't look like ladies' restrooms.

They had urinals, for one.

Surely that man would have noted the absence and realized he was in the wrong spot.

Normally she would have said the pink walls should have clued him in, but they weren't really pink; they were like a faded almost-beige color. They might have been pink at one time.

Her boys had disappeared, she assumed into bathroom stalls. If they thought it was odd to see a man in the ladies' restroom, it hadn't stopped them from going and doing what they needed to do, thankfully. The sooner they got that done, the sooner she could leave.

She shifted, adjusting her purse strap.

What did one say to a man when one met said man in the ladies' restroom?

Something told her she would not find suggestions for her current situation in an etiquette book.

After she was done raising her boys, maybe she would write an etiquette book for such situations in which she seemed to find herself at a loss.

Except she didn't know what she should say.

Her eyes narrowed. The man actually looked familiar.

He tilted his head, his face dimly lit by the fluttering light overhead, but his hat had moved enough for her to see the square jaw, bold nose, and the deep-set, dark blue eyes.

Yeah. Familiar.

There were a lot of Hudson boys in Cowboy Crossing, although all of them lived outside of town, and since she never had money to go anywhere, she hadn't seen any of them, other than occasionally running into someone at the grocery store or post office, in years.

Her husband had gone to the brick church in town, while the Hudson family went to the white one, so she didn't see him in church, either.

But she was pretty sure this was Zane. He'd always had more angular, serious, almost glowering facial features than his younger brothers. He'd been the serious brother. The bold one. The boss.

It was more than a dozen years ago when she'd practically been on her knees begging him for a favor, and he'd flatly refused.

She hadn't realized at the time that he had a confident and beautiful girlfriend from out east. It probably wouldn't have stopped her from asking him what she had.

His refusal had made her life take a turn for the worse.

"I think I know you?" His voice, low and soft, held just a hint of a question, but it also oozed with confidence. Zane had always been sure of himself.

She recognized the voice. Easily. "Zane. I wasn't expecting to meet you in here."

Maybe her face held humor. It probably did because seeing him had eased any worries about the truck stop. Zane might have refused her, but she didn't have to worry about anything happening to her while he was around. He was a good old boy in the best sense of the word, and it wouldn't even surprise her if he walked her out to her car, even though they really didn't know each other.

He'd probably heard her husband died. Cowboy Crossing was a small town, and news like that traveled. But she highly doubted she was at the top of anyone's list of most interesting people, and she couldn't imagine that Zane would care too much one way or the other about what happened to her.

Nothing had changed since high school in that regard.

This was probably only the third time she'd seen him in those dozen years and the first time she'd talked to him.

Maybe his lips twitched. She wasn't sure; it could have been the flickering light.

"My daughters had to use the restroom." His words felt a little abrupt, but maybe he was embarrassed because of where he was, which was somewhere he wasn't supposed to be.

Regardless, she dropped her eyes and fought the tightness of her throat. She wasn't the one in the wrong bathroom. She wasn't going to let his abrupt tone make her feel like she was the trespasser here.

"I'm pretty sure there are laws against this." She couldn't even believe she said that. She should be praising him for taking care of his daughters, not complaining that he was in her bathroom.

"Maybe there used to be." One of his brows went up, which made his expression kind of say that he might not completely agree with it, but he was taking advantage of it.

He was probably right. She was just having a knee-jerk reaction. She would never begrudge someone for taking care of their kids. After all, she had an eight-year-old in here, and he probably didn't belong any more than Zane did.

"This is a pretty rough place for you," Zane said, almost sounding normal. Like he talked to ladies in the ladies' restroom every day.

She was still sort of shocked and kind of embarrassed, and very, very thankful she didn't have to go. She would let her bladder explode before she would go into a stall with Zane standing right there.

Maybe that made her overly modest.

Or stupid.

She'd been called both and worse.

"I didn't realize this place was in such bad condition. I've never stopped here before. But I was supposed to be meeting someone down the road and needed gas." He didn't need to know how desperate she was.

His gaze sharpened when she said she was meeting someone. She thought about the parking lot and the rough-looking people at the back of it. It almost made her smile that Zane would think that she might be doing drugs, or other things, in the parking lot, bringing her kids along too.

He had a pretty low opinion of her, apparently.

But then his face relaxed, and he seemed to shake his head slightly. "You'll know not to stop here next time."

He didn't have a right to tell her what to do. What little she remembered from school, he had always been a commanding kind of person. She supposed it came from being the oldest of all those brothers. He'd always been very protective of his younger brothers, but he hadn't hesitated to tell them what to do either.

"That's a good idea. I think I'll do that." She didn't say that she'd already decided it. No point in wasting her breath. They'd walk out of this bathroom and not see each other for another twelve years. She didn't need to be his friend now. They were just making casual conversation between people who were very loose acquaintances.

Acquaintances, but she had heard he'd gotten divorced. She wasn't exactly in the grapevine of gossip, having been under Dexter's thumb since the day she'd said I do.

Then, in the year since his death, she'd been working even harder to try to keep things together. All in vain, probably.

The silence between them was getting awkward, and she couldn't think of anything to say. The last time they'd had any type of communication hung heavy between them, at least on her end. Maybe he didn't even remember.

He'd been in love with the eastern woman that he'd eventually married. She assumed that was the mother of his children and the woman from whom he'd gotten divorced. She'd heard that much about him anyway.

Thankfully, John came out of the stall just then, and she got ready to make sure he washed his hands. All her boys were old enough to do it themselves, but they hadn't gotten to the point where they believed they needed to.

She had just raised her brows at her son who had started to

bypass the sinks when a thundering crash coincided with the ground beneath her seeming to shake.

# Chapter Three

Waverley stumbled forward one step.

Zane reached out a hand and grabbed her shoulder even as he turned his eyes, scanning the stalls, as though looking for his girls.

Waverley's eyes went in the same direction.

John's face had turned toward them, and his mouth was an open "o," his gaze darting back and forth.

Little voices from inside stalls cried out, "Mommy? Mommy?"

Almost at the same time, she heard, "Daddy?" from two voices.

The lights, which had been flickering, shone brightly for half a second before they went out completely, leaving the restroom in pitch darkness—a thick darkness that felt unnatural for its deepness. Even a night with no moon or stars wasn't this dark.

"I'm right here. It's okay, honey. The lights just went out," she said in her most reassuring voice. The tone she might use to tell her boy he was going to be just fine even as she eyed the splintered bone sticking out from his skin.

She couldn't explain the big crash, but at least the ceiling wasn't falling down around them. She also thought the building was probably not on fire. All in all, she didn't feel like there was any need to panic, although there was definitely a part of her that wanted to give in to the clawing fear that scraped at the back of her throat. It had to be the darkness, so thick it could almost be felt. It was enough to give anybody a panic attack.

She couldn't indulge in that right now though. She had children who needed her.

"I suppose it could've been a bomb," Zane said beside her in a low tone. "But I think it might've been a truck ramming into the building. That seems more likely."

Waverley didn't realize she'd been holding her breath until she let it out at his words. A truck running into the building made a lot of sense.

"I'd better see if I can round up my boys."

"Do you want to stay here for a minute while I run out and make sure that's what happened?"

She didn't. Not really. The darkness felt like it was seeping into her skin, heavy and irritating.

"I can." She remembered the purse on her shoulder. Her cell phone was in it. She started digging, wanting light to push away the heavy feeling of the blackness around her.

"I'll just open the door and peek out." Zane shifted away from her, and his cell phone light came on. It shone at her feet first, giving her the light she needed to grab her own phone.

"Thank you."

"I won't be gone long. I'm not leaving the bathroom."

"That's fine." The red bar showed on her cell phone. The kids and she had been listening to music while they baked today, and she hadn't put her phone on the charger.

Still, she thought she had a charger in the car. Even if she didn't, it was worth running the battery down to get rid of the darkness.

"Daddy?"

"I'm right here, baby. I'm just going to stick my head out and make sure everything's okay outside. Be right back. The nice lady,

Mrs...." He paused, and Waverley assumed this was where she inserted her name.

She didn't really want to use her married name, so she simply said, "Waverley."

He hadn't remembered. Not that she thought he would. Why would he? She was the one who'd had a crush on him.

She wasn't the only one.

"Miss Waverley." His voice held a note of thanks. "I'm not leaving, I just want to make sure everything is safe."

He shifted away, and Waverley shivered from a sudden chill. Maybe she'd been depending more than she thought on his comforting presence beside her.

"It's dark in here. And I'm scared," a small voice said from the bathroom stall.

It was one of Zane's girls, but Waverley answered. "It's okay, sweetie. Daddy's right here, and I'll come over with my light." Waverley used the softest and sweetest voice she could manage. "What's your name, honey?"

"Ophelia," the girl said softly, with a little tremble in her voice.

"It's okay, Ophelia. I'm right here too. I'm stepping out of my stall which is right beside you. I'll be standing here when you get out." The voice belonged to a slightly older girl. If Waverley had to guess, she'd say maybe not quite teenage...ten or twelve.

"Thank you, honey. What's your name?" Waverley asked.

"Cordelia. From Shakespeare." The voice was matter-of-fact, like she was used to getting questions about her name.

"It's pretty. I like it. I don't know much about Shakespeare though. Maybe you can tell me about it sometime." She talked, keeping her voice soft and completely fear free, trying to make sure all the kids in the room stayed calm. As far as she knew, there wasn't anyone else aside from Zane and their children. So far, two girls and her three boys.

"Mommy? Where are you?" This came from Roman. She moved

down to where his voice came from as he said, "I can't get my stall open. I can't find the lock."

"I can do it, Mom," John volunteered, coming over beside her. "I can slide under the door. No problem."

"Hang on." She didn't want him to accidentally go into one of the girls' stalls. She tapped on the door. "Is this your stall, Roman?"

"I think so." He tapped back, and she assumed they had the right one.

She shone her light on the floor. "Go in this one," she said to John.

While she was waiting, footsteps echoed, muted clicks, sounding like work boots. Zane coming back.

She turned her head and focused on the light from his phone coming around the corner. Then she looked at his face and the outline from the glow of it.

"The door was jammed. It wasn't easy to get open to begin with, but whatever happened must have shifted the building. We're stuck in here for now. But I'm sure someone will be here to get us out shortly."

She supposed he said that last bit to calm everyone or to keep everyone from panicking. Or maybe just her, since his words had caused a shaft of the panic she'd been pushing back to cut loose and choke her windpipe.

She sucked in air, trying to open it back up. She was going to miss her rendezvous. The person she was meeting was on a tight schedule and wouldn't be waiting.

Also, her phone was going to go dead. On top of that, she could be stuck in the bathroom in the dark for who knew how long. The bathroom wasn't too bad, but she couldn't stand the dark.

"I'm calling someone right now, so people know we're here. I assume everyone's first inclination is going to be taking care of anyone who was hurt with whatever happened. I'd say we've got at least an hour in here. Although I'm not sure how they're going to get the door open."

"My phone's almost dead." Maybe that wasn't the most important thing she could say, but it was the one on her mind.

"Maybe you better turn it off then. Mine doesn't have a whole lot of life left on it either. I was at the sale, and I took a couple videos for my brothers and spent a lot of time talking on it. I didn't think to charge it in the truck on the way home. I guess one doesn't really think that they're going to end up stuck in a bathroom in the dark." His light snuffed off too. "I'm going to make a few calls then shut it off."

She called and left a message for the person she was supposed to be meeting. He continued to make some calls while the kids came out of the stalls. She used the glow from his phone to make sure everyone's hands got washed, although she wasn't sure what good that was going to do if they were all stuck in here.

"This is pretty cool. Stuck in the bathroom." John's voice shook, not with fear but with excitement. Leave it to a little boy to think this was a great adventure.

Waverley wasn't going to correct him in the notion, either. "I'm going to be over here against the wall. I know you're not going to want to, but come over here and sit down. You might hurt yourself walking into something in the dark, and we have no way of getting you out of here to take care of you. Or you might run into someone else, too."

"That sounds reasonable. Cordelia and Ophelia, you guys better do the same."

"I just want to come over and hold your hand, Daddy." Ophelia's squeaky voice came from the sink where she'd just finished washing her hands.

"How about I come over and get you?"

The air beside her stirred, and Zane moved away.

Waverley told herself she didn't care where he ended up. She'd already said where she was going to be, so she put her back against the wall and slid down, sitting on the floor and trying not to be grossed out by how dirty the bathroom floor had been when she'd seen it under the light.

She would make her boys take a shower and wash their clothes, and all the dirt would be gone. She tried to tell herself that, although she'd rather be sitting down outside on the ground. Somehow, it just seemed cleaner.

She had to admit she was a little surprised when Zane came back, his heavier, thicker footsteps accompanied by the soft little clicks of his daughter. His phone turned on and pointed in her direction. She couldn't really see his face, but he moved some more, clicking it off before he ended up sliding down the wall and sitting beside her with maybe three feet between them.

"Mind if I join you?"

She smiled at the humor in his voice. She supposed she could play along, if being a little funny was what he was doing, although it seemed unlikely.

"I'd be happy to have you. Make yourself at home."

"This truck stop is nothing like home. Sorry."

They were going to be stuck together for a while, so she might as well push the hurt and disappointment from her rejection years ago aside and do her best to make some casual conversation.

"Do you still live in Cowboy Crossing?" She thought she knew the answer to that question, but she really hadn't gotten out much since her marriage, then the death of her husband.

"I have a farm outside of town. Not far. I just bought the neighbor's place, and a week ago, I got custody of my girls."

That seemed like an awful long answer to the question she'd asked. Maybe the dark loosened his mouth. She didn't remember him as someone who talked a lot.

His voice came out of the darkness, like he'd decided it was his turn to ask about her. "I'm pretty sure you live in town somewhere. Remember hearing your husband died a year ago or so."

"That's right. It's been about sixteen months. He died last November."

Zane grunted. "Sorry."

It was on the tip of Waverley's tongue to say, "I'm not." But she didn't want to speak badly of the dead. He'd provided for her, and she was grateful. She also had six boys because of him, and she wouldn't trade them for anything either.

"Kind of funny you have boys, and I have girls. Sometimes the Lord's sense of humor is a bit more than I can understand."

She saw the reasoning in that. One would have thought God would have given her girls if he was going to take her husband and would have given Zane boys if he was going to get custody of his kids.

"Things usually don't happen the way we think they should." She didn't know what else to say. She knew for a fact that was true. "You said you just got custody?"

"Last week. It's been an adjustment."

She could imagine. Girls could be difficult to get used to. Although Ophelia was young enough that she would probably just be sweet. It was the older girl who was most likely giving him fits.

"I'm sure your mother will help you." Everyone in Cowboy Crossing knew Mrs. Hudson. Waverley had grown up in the same church, but when she married Dexter, she'd started going to his and kind of lost touch with Mrs. Hudson.

"She will. She's offered. But I fought so long and so hard for this, I hate to give any of it up. If she watches them, she likes to do it at her house."

"It's going to be really hard for you to be a full-time farmer and a full-time father as well. Especially with Ophelia."

"I know."

"But Cordelia looks like she's old enough to keep an eye on her sister for a while after school."

A breath huffed out of the darkness. "That's what Mom said you were going to do. She said I'll be a slave at your house and all I'll ever do will be to keep an eye on—"

"That's enough." The volume of Zane's voice hadn't changed, but there was a hard edge there.

Cordelia snapped her mouth closed immediately. Waverley could hear her teeth clack together.

That would be hard, having the kids with their mom and then trying to take them on himself. She admired him for wanting them. There was probably a story behind it, but she didn't figure he'd want to tell it in front of the children.

Surprising her, her boys had all settled down around her, and even Roman didn't chatter like he usually did. He sat in her lap with his head on her shoulder.

She thought, but she wasn't sure, that Cordelia was sitting on the other side of Zane. Ophelia had settled in his lap.

"Are we ever going to get out of here?" Ax asked in a trembling voice.

She moved her right arm and put it around him, pulling him into her side.

"Of course we are. It's just a matter of waiting for a bit."

Maybe the fear in Ax's voice had upset Roman, because he seemed to try to snuggle down further into her lap. She tightened her grip on him even as John lay his head on her left arm.

She didn't have her guitar, but she'd often sat with her children in the evening in their room and sang songs with them before she read them a story. It had always been up to her to do bedtime, because Dexter wouldn't be moved from in front of the TV. Other than wishing the kids could see their dad before bed, she really didn't mind. She'd made a nice routine which she really enjoyed thinking about now.

She wished for her guitar but figured she could sing just as well without it.

Maybe Zane would think she was nuts, but singing might help Ophelia feel better too. Thinking she would start out with something upbeat and fun, she sang a couple of children's songs.

As soon as she started, she realized that singing in the bathroom was almost like singing in the shower. The acoustics made her voice echo. The boys joined in, kind of sleepily.

Maybe she should have started with something a little slower, because it was past their bedtime.

She was trying to think of something to sing after she'd sung the last line of another children's song, but then Zane's deep voice started, which surprised her. He sang the first few words before she joined him in harmony.

*What a friend we have in Jesus,*
*All our sins and griefs to bear!*
*What a privilege to carry*
*Everything to God in prayer!*

The music seemed to form a bubble or shield around them, enclosing them all in the same safe space and chasing out the shadows from inside. It was still just as dark in the bathroom, but she didn't feel the darkness in her soul anymore.

*Oh, what peace we often forfeit,*
*Oh, what needless pain we bear,*
*All because we do not carry*
*Everything to God in prayer!*

If Matthew and Mark were there, they would sing harmony with her on the chorus, which was what they did in the car to pass the time when they had a long ride.

Zane started on the second verse, and the words came easily to her lips, too.

*Have we trials and temptations?*
*Is there trouble anywhere?*
*We should never be discouraged—*
*Take it to the Lord in prayer.*

She had never considered herself a great singer, and she'd always had her guitar to accompany her, but she was able to hold the melody as Zane sang harmony on the next lines.

*Can we find a friend so faithful,*
*Who will all our sorrows share?*
*Jesus knows our every weakness;*
*Take it to the Lord in prayer.*

It surprised her when Cordelia started with a strong soprano. After a moment, Waverley dropped down in harmony, and Zane sang bass.

*Are we weak and heavy-laden,*
*Cumbered with a load of care?*
*Precious Savior, still our refuge—*
*Take it to the Lord in prayer.*

Singing made her forget about the darkness. It also seemed to bond them together, making it feel like they were close and not stranded alone in the darkness. Her spirits lifted as they sang, finishing the last few lines of the song in sweet harmony.

*Do thy friends despise, forsake thee?*
*Take it to the Lord in prayer!*
*In His arms He'll take and shield thee,*
*Thou wilt find a solace there.*

As the last note trailed off, peace seemed to settle down like a soft blanket in the friendly darkness.

Waverley smiled. Funny how singing could do that.

The right song probably had something to do with it.

Part of her brain wanted to go down the trail of wondering what it would have been like to be married to a godly man who would think to sing hymns while they were trapped in the bathroom. But that way just lay dissatisfaction with the lot that she'd been given in life—the lot that she'd chosen. So she shut it down, grateful that if she had to be stuck in the ladies' restroom with a man, that man was

Zane.

What were the odds?

If she would have had to pick a man to walk in on in the ladies' restroom, Zane would not have been at the top of the list. He wouldn't have been on the list at all.

# Chapter Four

Zane started a few more songs, hymns, soft and slow ones, just hoping that maybe it would be enough to lure the children into sleep. By the time they'd sung five or six, even Cordelia was snoring.

Waverley sang beautiful harmony with him. He forgot how much he enjoyed singing. He'd sung with his family growing up, but Vicki had never been interested, even though she had a beautiful voice. It was boring for her, he supposed, while he enjoyed blending his voice in the evening air after a hard day of work. Just relaxing and uplifting in a way that nothing else could compare.

But he'd been fine with her desire to do other things, had been happy about it, as long as she stayed true. Until she strayed.

No looking back.

He could enjoy this moment, even if he was sitting on a hard bathroom floor and even if he did feel like a failure as a father because he somehow managed to get his daughters stuck in the bathroom.

"I didn't want to say this while the kids were awake, but when I talked to someone on the phone, they said it was going to be a while.

The person I talked to said they would try to figure out how to open it safely and that it probably would not be before morning, but as long as we were comfortable and no one was hurt, they were going to put the emphasis on safety rather than speed."

"That makes sense. Thanks for telling me. I guess we're sleeping in here tonight."

"The kids are sleeping anyway. Kind of doubting that I'll be getting many Zs leaning against the wall and sitting on the floor."

She made a little noise, almost a "hmm," but didn't say anything more.

He'd heard a little about her over the years, mostly about her husband not being a good man, which had made a small part of him sad. She'd not been a raving beauty in school, and he'd never been interested, but he wouldn't wish a jerk husband on anyone.

He hadn't known she had three children. Three boys.

Thankfully, she'd been good with his girls. She'd gotten Cordelia to talk, which was more than he could do most of the time.

He wondered if she would be interested in a job.

She didn't seem like a horrible person to hang around, and he enjoyed singing with her. As far as he knew, she had a good reputation.

"Who are you meeting?" he asked as a way of making conversation while he considered the idea that had sprung into his head—she could be a nanny for him.

"Someone who ordered baked goods. That's what I do. Cook—mostly desserts—and sell them."

He couldn't imagine she made much. That would be a lot of work, too. She seemed tired.

"That probably takes a lot of time."

"It does. Thursday and Friday are busy because I sell a lot of stuff on the weekend."

"Makes sense." He figured it wouldn't hurt to come right out and just lay out his situation. Maybe she'd be interested. "You were right when you said that it was going to take a lot for me to be a full-time father and a full-time farmer. I was actually thinking that I needed to find a nanny or housekeeper or something."

"I think that's a good idea." Her voice was kinda subdued, like she didn't really care whether he found a housekeeper or nanny or not and she was just making polite conversation.

He couldn't blame her. That's probably how he'd sound if she were talking about her personal issues.

He'd discovered that she had a crush on him when they were in their twenties and she'd come to his mother's house and, out of the total blue, asked him to marry her. He'd been completely shocked, since he'd barely remembered her name.

Of course, he'd said "no" and gone on to marry Vicki.

Big mistake.

He wondered what would have happened if he'd answered her differently. At the time, he'd been enamored with Vicki, convinced that they were meant to be together.

Vicki was flashy, confident, a go-getter. Perfect hair and career. He'd never met anyone like her, and she'd captivated him from the first.

Looking back, someone like Waverley would've made a much better wife. Someone steady and content. Someone who was good with kids, loyal. She'd stayed with her jerk husband, anyway.

Vicki didn't have a loyal bone in her body.

He'd figured that out too late.

"Do you know anyone who would be interested?" It wasn't the question he wanted to ask her, but he didn't know how to come right out and say *would you be interested in a job?* It just seemed too... blunt.

"As a nanny? Or housekeeper? Or the combination of both?" Her voice was soft, and she shifted. He realized now that the soft yeast and cinnamon and moonlight stroll scent that he'd been smelling wasn't the harsh chemical scent of a bathroom air freshener. It was softer and sweeter. Waverley. He liked it.

"I really want a combination. Someone who will watch the girls after school, then cook supper. Maybe be there in the morning to get them up for school and dressed. Maybe do a little light housework, laundry. Someone who will help them with homework if I'm not there. And get them to bed at a decent hour, especially in the spring when I have to start planting and in the fall during harvest."

"Basically, you want a wife." Waverley's voice could have held bitterness, but he thought it was humor. He could hear her smile.

She was right.

A wife might not be a bad idea. Except he had no prospects. He'd been married, then spent so much time fighting for custody that he couldn't drag another woman into that and honestly didn't want to. The whole experience had soured him on women. He'd thought Vicki was everything she appeared to be, and it had turned out that she was nothing like she seemed.

Not doing that again.

Except...

His head turned, but he couldn't see anything in the black darkness. He wanted to run his eyes over her hair, see her features.

He could see the picture in his mind as she walked into the bathroom. Her eyes big as saucers, her mouth open, shocked at seeing a man in the ladies' room.

Her hair had been dark brown and piled on top of her head. He guessed it was past her shoulders, but he didn't know much about women's hair. Her face wasn't strikingly beautiful as Vicki's had been, but he'd noticed from the first the humor in her eyes. She'd had a quirky little smile on, despite her shock seeing him.

She didn't have a girl's skinny figure, but for having three boys, she seemed slender and fit. Not that any of that would make a difference.

He liked her voice. He liked how she treated his girls. He liked the fact that he knew that she'd been loyal to her husband even though he hadn't been kind to her.

Why not?

"I guess I *am* looking for a wife. Kinda hard to do any dating with kids." There, he'd hinted it would be hard for them to date. Maybe she would catch his insinuation.

"True."

No. She definitely didn't catch it, or else she completely ignored it. He was really bad at beating around the bush. He'd always been better at just throwing things out there. Giving commands and expecting them to be followed.

This probably wasn't the type of subject that worked with his kind of personality. As the darkness settled between them, deepening somehow, he didn't know how else to do it.

"Do you make very much selling baked goods?" Nosy. Not what he intended.

She answered anyway. "Enough. Enough to pay the rent and buy groceries. Usually. Except when things break down, or except when one of my boys steps on a nail and I have to pay the emergency room to take it out."

"Oh. That sounds painful."

"I think it probably was. But the emergency room had morphine, and I didn't. So it was worth the money."

"Then you couldn't make the rent?"

"No."

"What are you going to do?"

"I don't know. I guess I'll be evicted. But until then, I'll work my butt off trying to catch up. It just seems like it's impossible because every time I think I've got it under control, something unexpected comes up. I guess that's where I trust the Lord that He's got something planned since I have no idea."

"Sometimes God's plans are odd. Not what we expect. Not something we would've thought of on our own." There. That was him beating around the bush.

"That's true. You're absolutely right."

"I think I have an idea that might possibly be one of God's odd plans for you. And one that would help me as well."

"Well, this is a good time to talk about it. We're unlikely to be interrupted, and neither one of us is going anywhere."

She seemed totally unaware that he was about to propose a marriage of convenience.

Maybe he was crazy for even thinking it, but it wouldn't be too bad.

He wasn't in any danger of falling in love with her. But she seemed like she'd make a nice friend. After Vicki, he valued loyalty and faithfulness far above looks or social status. Waverley definitely possessed both in abundance.

Seven children between them. His four and her three. That was a lot of kids, but they could make it work. Before he talked himself out of it, his mouth opened.

"Would you marry me?"

If the darkness had been silent and deep before, it grew bigger now and expanded, sucking them both in, chewing them up, and spitting them out.

Maybe he was being a little dramatic. But it did seem difficult to breathe as the seconds ticked on and on.

He was about to backpedal, say he was just goofing, or make a joke out of it—he was rolling words over in his mind, trying to figure out how to get out of it with the least embarrassment possible—when her voice broke through the stillness.

"Okay."

# Chapter Five

Was she nuts?

What had she just agreed to?

Zane had probably been kidding, and she had taken him seriously. Now he was probably trying to figure out how to make it less awkward. Maybe she should.

But marrying Zane would solve her problems. It would provide a father for her boys, and she wouldn't be evicted. Child services wouldn't come and take her children. And yeah, she assumed he basically wanted her to do slave labor at his house for no pay. Well, a roof over her head and a roof over her children's heads and enough food to keep them from going hungry was pay enough.

She could still do her baking on the side. Maybe she'd end up with a little bit of extra spending money so he wouldn't have to buy her kids clothes, and maybe she could contribute to the groceries as well.

She'd never driven a tractor or anything like that, so she'd be no help out in the field. But she could find things to do to make herself useful. He would be getting a good bargain for the most part. Her thoughts kind of stopped there, because she wasn't sure how much of a real marriage Zane was expecting, if he hadn't been joking.

Eight kids would be a lot, but they could do it. His two and her six.

"What?" he asked.

Had she misheard? Surely she hadn't dreamed it? In the darkness, everything seemed weird.

If she'd heard correctly, it felt like a risk worth taking. She hadn't taken too many risks in her life, and she didn't necessarily think that risks were good. But this one could turn out to be; she just had a feeling. She also had a peace about it that was unexpected but welcome.

"I said okay." She waited three seconds and then said, "Does that surprise you?"

"Yeah," he said immediately. Then he cleared his throat. "I mean, it did...I guess. It surprised me that I even asked."

"It surprised me too. But it actually makes sense to me. I can see everything working out in my head, but if you change your mind, it's no big deal. It's not like I'm emotionally invested in it. It just seems like a good solution for both of us."

Unlike the last time she had been begging him to marry her. She'd definitely been emotionally invested then, although part of that had been because she didn't want to have to marry Dexter.

It was impossible that he could read her mind, but he did surprise her when he said, "It's been over a decade since you asked me to marry you."

His words were hesitant and kind of hung in the air. She wished she could brush them away, like they'd never been said. Of course, that was impossible, but she didn't say anything in reply. It wasn't her best day and definitely wasn't one of her best memories.

Like he didn't notice that his choice of subject had made her wish she were trapped with anyone else, he kept speaking in a thoughtful tone. "I didn't think too much about it for the first few years, but Vicki turned out to be a really bad decision, and I wondered at times how things might have been different if I hadn't been blindly stupid and had thought about picking someone..." His words trailed off.

She figured she knew what he was going to say. She waited, but he never finished.

He probably didn't want to insult her, so she suggested, "Someone you didn't love? Someone you weren't attracted to? Someone who was just the commonsense choice?"

"Yeah."

All those things hurt.

She wanted him to be attracted to her. She wanted him to admire her like she had admired him. Still did really. Not just because he was good-looking, but she knew he was honest and a hard worker. Kind. Maybe bossy, but not mean like Dexter had been.

There was a lot to admire in Zane.

Definitely, having him love her was more than she could hope for. After all, she had never been under the illusion that she loved him, either. She didn't really know him.

"Sometimes, I think the way we go about choosing a spouse in our modern society is about the stupidest way anybody could do it." She meant that. Not that that was the way that she had chosen hers. Her parents had pretty much said Dexter was what they wanted her to do, and she could either accept his proposal or they were going to kick her out of the house.

She hadn't been prepared for that.

In hindsight, she should have just left home and struck out on her own. It couldn't have been worse. But she'd been raised to be a good daughter and had never given her parents a spot of trouble.

If she hadn't done what they wanted, she wouldn't have her boys.

If Zane had anything to add to that, he didn't. Rather, he changed the subject. "I suppose, if you're serious, because I actually think I am, we should hash out the details. Expectations maybe?"

"That makes sense." It was sensible. She could add that to his list of virtues.

Dexter hadn't had common sense either. She wanted to stop

comparing the two. She didn't want to spend the rest of her life holding Zane up to Dexter.

Dexter would come out looking bad every time.

"What are your expectations?" she asked.

"I guess I laid them out earlier. I want a mother for my girls, and someone to help feed and clothe them, to help them with schoolwork, and to do the housework and anything that needs done around the farm, pitching in and lending a hand with it.

"In return, I'll provide, protect, and make sure we have a stable home for all of our children."

It seemed like she was doing a lot of work, but he hadn't listed his work other than providing for her, which would probably involve a lot of mornings getting up before the sun and coming back into the house at dark.

"Do you have expectations?" he asked, almost hesitantly.

———

For the first time since the lights went out, Zane was thankful for the deep darkness.

What had he done?

It probably wasn't too late to take it back. To make it seem like a joke. To say *that was a bad idea, let's forget it.*

But he found he really didn't want to.

This—this crazy idea—solved everything.

Waverley was a nice lady. Steadfast. He knew that much from her marriage. He didn't really know any details, other than her husband hadn't been kind, yet she'd stuck with him anyway. If she'd do it for that man, she'd probably do it for Zane too.

He wouldn't have to worry about having her up and decide she was going to leave and take his kids someday.

It was his biggest issue: trust.

Not that he would give Waverley unconditional trust, because he wouldn't. He didn't think he'd ever be able to give unconditional trust again. But as women went, she wasn't like Vicki.

"I suppose we ought to have some ground rules. That seems like a good idea." Although her voice was soft, it held steel, something he'd noticed from the beginning.

In high school, he remembered her as kind of timid, maybe even mousy. Boring. She had her nose in a book and walked around the halls with her books clutched to her chest and staring at the ground.

Even her hair had been a brownish, mousy color.

There was nothing striking about her features, either. Nothing that would make her stand out.

Somewhere along the way, she'd developed that core of steel. Or maybe she'd always had it, and he had never taken the time to actually see it.

He thought again of the day that she begged him to marry her. He'd been flabbergasted.

He'd barely even known she was alive and probably couldn't have said her name without thinking about it, despite the small school. He certainly hadn't been thinking of love or of dating her, and definitely not of marriage.

He hadn't wanted to laugh in her face, and he'd rejected her as gently as possible, but the idea had been preposterous. To him anyway.

After hearing about her marriage and listening to some of the town gossip—someday maybe he'd get the whole story—he could see that she'd been desperate. But he'd fancied himself in love with someone else and hadn't even given the idea any consideration or merit.

Now, in an ironic twist, he'd just asked *her* to marry *him*.

That's where the irony had ended though, because she'd said yes.

Now she wanted ground rules.

It was a shock that he was even considering a marriage of convenience. Thirty minutes ago, the idea was not even in his head. Now he needed to come up with ground rules.

"Do you have any ideas?"

There. He'd just lobbed the ball back onto her side of the net.

"We each need to treat the other's children equally."

He liked that that was the first thing she thought of. The children. Although he didn't know what else he was expecting. But according to the person he'd talked with on the phone, they'd be stuck here for a while and would have some time to think about it.

"I agree. I don't give my kids special treatment, and you don't give yours special treatment, either." He stroked Ophelia's head, which rested against his diaphragm, fingering her baby-fine hair. It was shorter than all of her sisters' and felt thin.

He hadn't spent much time with his daughters and even less touching his little girl's head. It was amazing to him that this was actually his daughter.

Before he got caught up in that, he said, "I suppose we should write this stuff down and take it to a lawyer and have them draw up some kind of agreement."

"If that's what you feel we need. I feel like if I say I'm going to do it, I'll do it. I'd like to think I can trust you the same way."

Red flags went up all over the place for him. Vicki would say that: "Don't you trust me?"

He supposed, looking back, the question had been designed to make him feel guilty for distrusting her. However, it had turned out he'd been right to distrust her, because she'd been lying to him almost from the beginning. Starting with Cordelia. He hadn't known that she was pregnant with another man's child when they got married.

"I think I'd feel better if we have a lawyer involved."

"Okay." If she were disappointed, he couldn't really tell by the tone of her voice. But he could almost feel something between them, something that seemed to radiate off her. Like she'd hoped that there could be that bond of trust between them.

After Vicki, not likely.

He did appreciate her easy capitulation on a point that he'd wanted. It made him feel like he might need to give in to her. He wasn't used to giving in. Maybe from being the oldest in the family, but he'd rather command than obey or follow.

"So our kids are equal. What else?" he asked.

"Your turn." Again, there was that steel in her voice. Determination. She would capitulate, but not because she couldn't win. Sometimes, it took a stronger person to give in than it did to fight.

"I already pledged to provide for you. House, money for groceries, clothes, and extra. Anything over a certain amount, we probably ought to agree to spend. If you want to be involved in the farm finances, you can. But I don't want joint checking accounts."

Maybe he sounded a little more forceful than was strictly necessary, but that was another area where he'd been burned by Vicki. She'd taken all the money from the account they shared. Thankfully, she'd never had her name added to the farm account. Although Jane, a teller down at the bank, told him later that Vicki had tried to get Jane to transfer money from the farm account into the account she'd drained.

"That's fine. A separate account for the farm, with just you. A joint household account, with both of us, and I'll keep the account I have with just me. That's where any money I make from my baked goods goes. And that's where I'll take the expenses from for my baking."

"Is that a business account?"

"Yes."

Perfect. They had the money issue straightened out. Separate accounts, with a joint account for the household expenses. Money and trust. It all tied in with not being able to trust her.

Maybe he wasn't being very fair to Waverley. Actually, he was sure he wasn't being fair to Waverley. Maybe he should give her an explanation, but he didn't really want to. Not now.

"What else?" he asked.

"You said you would provide a house and living expenses. In return, I'll take care of the household chores, even if it's by assigning responsibilities to each child—equally, of course—and I'll make sure the cooking and cleaning and washing get done. I'll take the main responsibility for the children." Here she paused.

He waited. From the tone of her voice, it was obvious there was more she wanted to say, and he'd found that normally it was best to just wait and let people talk.

After what felt like a long time, or maybe it was just the darkness, she finally started. "But I don't want to be a single mother when it comes to the kids."

He couldn't blame her. With her three and his four, seven kids was a lot for one person to be responsible for.

He had to be honest with her. "There's gonna be some times of the year—planting and harvesting in particular, haying in the summer —when I'm going to be gone from daylight until dark. In the summer, that's a good sixteen, eighteen hours. You might be a single mom for those times of the year. But I promise, the rest of the time, I want to be a dad. I don't know that I'll be a very good one, I don't seem to have been very successful this last week, but I promise that I'll try, and I'll do the best I can."

He couldn't promise more. And honestly, since he wasn't trusting her, he couldn't expect her to believe his promise. He probably should make sure that went on the lawyer's papers too.

"Fair enough."

It bothered him a little how she seemed to accept his words so easily. He could be lying to her. Why was she being so gullible? He could take her to the cleaners. Except she didn't have anything.

Nothing other than herself and her kids, which she was completely trusting him with. He should really give her a hard time about that, but it made him want to become the man she already thought he was.

He didn't want to disappoint her.

But he wasn't doing this without a lawyer.

"I have the farm that I bought fifteen years ago and the one that I just bought a couple of months ago. That's a lot of land, and that's a lot of money. I want a prenup. If you stay with me, it can be ours, but if you leave, you're not taking the farm too. I'm not paying you for what I already have." His words were rough, and he felt bad about that, a little. But he was serious, because he'd already paid for his farm twice. When he'd bought it and when Vicki had left.

"I'm not leaving."

There was that soft voice of steel wrapped in sweetness. He would believe her, except he'd heard it before.

His breath came harder and faster. He took a deep one, filling his lungs, to ease the irritation that scratched under the skin on his chest.

"No offense, but that's what my first wife said too." He couldn't keep from gritting his jaw. "Forgive me for not believing it."

He could almost feel her drawing away from him. It was probably a good thing he hadn't had to court her, or anyone, because even he could see that his words were pushing her away rather than cementing a bond between them, becoming something that would make them stronger as a married couple.

Which kind of brought him to what was probably the elephant in the room: would this be a "real" marriage?

He supposed, if it wasn't, he would be better served just hiring a nanny or housekeeper or both. The problem was where would he find them? And how could he find someone he could trust with his children?

Waverley needed a home; he was in a position to provide it, since he lived in a six-bedroom farmhouse. There was plenty of room for her three children and his four. But he couldn't live with her and not be married to her.

What exactly did that mean?

What did he want?

He had an idea, but maybe he'd better figure out what she was thinking. It would probably be the most awkward thing they had to talk about.

He listened to the sounds of their children. Two of them were snoring at jarringly different times. Cordelia had just settled closer to him, stirring in her sleep, but from her deep breathing, she was completely out.

He thought it safe to discuss without little ears hearing.

For him, it had always been best to be blunt. He couldn't see doing anything else now. "Are we going to share a bedroom?"

He congratulated himself on the unemotional nature of those words. He could've asked her if they should paint the kitchen green. He'd done well.

But beside him, she almost seemed to shrink back. Like his words hadn't been the resounding success that he considered them. Like they might've...hurt...or maybe not the words. Maybe it was the way he said them. Should he have said them differently?

They needed to talk about it, and it seemed like the less emotion they had in the situation, the better.

Some of the steel had gone out of her voice when she answered. "I assumed that you could find a housekeeper or a nanny who would not share your bedroom. But a wife, on the other hand, would."

Though her voice was soft, he almost felt like he'd been dressed down, except her tone hadn't contained any censor. It was possibly just as unemotional as his, only there was a vulnerability there that had replaced the steel.

"I suppose you're right." Again, his words were terse, matter-of-fact.

Probably that had to do with Vicki, too. There'd been something that happened to him when he'd realized that he hadn't been enough for her. If that's what it was. Maybe she just fell out of love.

Whatever it was, the fact that she needed to go to someone else had hurt his pride. Not that he would ever admit it to anyone, not even to himself most of the time. But that wound was deep and gaping and would probably never heal.

He wasn't the kind of person that sat around asking himself what was wrong with him. Why didn't she love him? Why hadn't he been able to keep his wife?

But there was definitely a pride thing, where he felt lesser somehow, because she had gone, leaving the impression that he'd been lacking in some way.

How could he believe any different?

It'd been hard to face people in the town, whether they were chuckling behind their hands or not. Whether their sympathy was sincere... Either way, it had been hard.

"We might as well put that in the lawyer's contract. If you're going to cheat on me, tell me first and move out. You don't need to do it while you're living under my roof." Again, his words came out harsher than he'd intended, but he couldn't regret it. Better he showed harshness than the pain that still lurked in his chest.

Not pain because he was pining over Vicki. Pain that he wasn't good enough, that he couldn't keep his wife happy, and that he probably couldn't keep the next one happy either.

"As long as I'm living there, it will be *our* roof. And you can put it in if you want. It's unnecessary."

Her words made him feel small in a way, but still, he felt justified. Nothing was worse than going through that heartache again.

"It's going in. Don't you want the same thing about me?"

"No. I know you would never do that."

Again, her rock-solid faith in him bothered him. Had she not ever lived in the world? Didn't she know that this happened all the time? People didn't keep their word? How could she just lay herself open like that and give him the opportunity to cheat and hurt her? She should be protecting herself, not trusting him.

"I'll put it in. You need to have some protections too."

"Don't put it in. I don't want it." She shifted, which he sensed more than felt, since they weren't touching. "I trust you. I'll be vowing to stay with you until death, and you're going to do the same. That's enough for me."

Some part of him admired that, because that's the way it was supposed to be. The rings and the vows were unbreakable promises before an Almighty God, but that's not the way the world worked anymore.

"I still think you should have it in. It's protection for you."

Again, he could feel some kind of emotion coming off her, hitting him, pushing and sliding in the dark. He couldn't name it, but he could feel it almost like a physical touch. Not a pleasant one.

She spoke again; this time, steel was all he heard. "Are you saying you're going to cheat on me? Are you worried that you are?"

"Of course not."

"I know you're not. I don't need it in writing."

His guilt almost choked him. Guilt that he'd placed so little trust in her, while she was placing so much in him. But as much as he wanted to open his mouth and say "I don't need to put it in either, because I trust you too," he just couldn't. After what Vicki had done, after the fights, and the years, and the lawyers, and the lies, and the pain...after all that, how could he trust someone else?

*Because Waverley isn't Vicki,* a small voice said.

He knew that. Of course, he knew that. He'd just been thinking that very thing—that he would have been smarter to go with Waverley rather than Vicki because they were different. But still...

He also wasn't in love with Waverley. Not that he was sure that he had actually been in love with Vicki. Maybe he'd mistaken infatuation with real love. Or maybe he had been in love, and she'd killed it. Beaten it to death with her cheating and her lying and her lawyers and her insults and her selfish disregard of him as a father when she tried to take his girls and keep them away from him. There's no way love could have survived all of that.

And there's no way he would want to go through that again.

Waverley was the perfect person for him to marry, because he didn't love her and never would.

# Chapter Six

Three days later, Waverley sat in the passenger seat of Zane's pickup, twisting the ring on her finger as they came back from the church where Zane's brother, Deacon, had just married them.

Deacon's wife, Blair—now her sister-in-law—had been their witness.

It hadn't entirely surprised her, because she knew Zane was a no-nonsense kind of man, that they had made the decision to get married and three days later it was done.

They'd gotten out of the truck stop okay. It'd been about four o'clock in the morning when safety crews had decided that the building wasn't going to fall down if they pried the bathroom door open.

Zane had been right; a truck had smashed into it.

From what Waverley understood, the guy was drunk enough that he probably didn't feel a thing, although he was taken to the emergency room for multiple fractures. He was the only one hurt. Thankfully.

Zane had apparently gone to the lawyer the next day, and that afternoon, he'd arrived with a piece of paper for her to look over. The following day, they'd signed and notarized it, and today, she had dropped her kids off at his house with his mother.

When she'd arrived, he'd been out in the barn, already changed but checking on a cow that he had freshening.

She had the feeling he didn't want to leave the cow, but when she'd shown up, he'd come out and waited for her at his pickup.

"I never thought to ask if there was anything you needed in town. We could have gotten our joint account set up too. Sorry. I guess I just have that cow on my mind. She lost her calf last time, and I want to make sure I'm around in case she has trouble this time."

"I understand."

She did. Truly. She'd grown up in Missouri around farmers and cowboys. She knew cows were money, and a man was only as good as he treated his animals.

She couldn't blame him, and she wasn't upset about that.

She did, however, wonder if she wasn't making a poor decision.

To Zane, this was pure business, and he'd been very clear about that in the restroom as they'd talked.

She, on the other hand, already had feelings involved. She wasn't head over heels in love with him, but she supposed she could be. Her. Not him.

And there was the rub. Was she giving up the chance that she maybe could find someone who might be able to love her?

Was there a chance for that?

She had six children. What were the odds that some man would look at her and her six kids and want to take them all?

Zane had at least taken on that much.

Still, it had hurt her feelings that he hadn't made any bones about the fact that he wasn't attracted to her and didn't care if he'd be sharing a bedroom with her.

It wasn't a tit for tat. She'd been married long enough to Dexter to know that marriage couldn't be a tit for tat, that relationships in general couldn't be a tit for tat or they just ended up spiraling downward.

Someone had to be willing to give more, because relationships were more like a seesaw. Sometimes one person gave more, sometimes the other person did. If they were like a balanced weight, life would be perfect. And if there was one thing that she knew, and she knew she didn't know much, it was that life wasn't perfect. Ever.

"You didn't have much time in the house. Did you figure out the bedroom situation for the kids so they can get their stuff unpacked and settled?"

"No. I wasn't upstairs." She'd talked to his mother some. Although, it seemed like an awful lot of kids were running around, and she assumed Mrs. Hudson had brought some cousins with her.

They hadn't needed to talk much for her to see that Mrs. Hudson was just as wonderful as she remembered, but the older woman had stumbled when she'd mentioned Zane's dad, which gave Waverley the idea that maybe Mr. Hudson wasn't all on board with Zane up and marrying a woman he'd met in a truck stop bathroom three days prior.

Not that anyone in the world would blame him.

That definitely seemed like something only a romance novelist with an overactive imagination would dream up. Not something that would actually happen to someone in real life.

Sometimes truth was stranger than fiction.

She twisted the ring again, surprised that Zane had even thought to get them. But he'd come with one for her and one for him.

Maybe Deacon had reminded him. Deacon seemed like the kind of guy who would say something about rings when Zane asked if he'd marry him to a stranger.

She supposed, like every other girl, she used to dream about her wedding. Now she'd had two, neither one of them fancy.

Zane flipped the turn signal on as they approached his long driveway.

Their driveway. Waverley's stomach fisted, and she was glad

she'd not eaten anything. Things would settle down, and she'd get used to them.

Tilting her eyes over, she admired Zane's hands, which were sure on the wheel. He drove like he lived, with confidence and without apology.

She'd done a dangerous thing today. For her. She'd done a wonderful thing for her boys—that much she was totally sure of.

But Zane...

She admired him. Always had. And she liked him too.

Unfortunately, he seemed to be able to either take her or leave her.

Maybe, if it hadn't been so enticing to have a roof over her head that she didn't have to worry about every day and to have a good father for her boys, she wouldn't have done what she did.

Part of her scoffed at that though. Zane was a catch. She was blessed to have him.

*You're a catch, too*, a little voice in her head said.

Ha. Maybe.

Dexter wouldn't say so. She'd spent a lot of years thinking he was right.

In the year that he'd been gone, she'd kind of started coming into her own, no longer under her father's or husband's thumb. Now she'd gone back to where she'd been.

She didn't have to be what she used to be.

"I assume the bags which are still in the back of the truck are yours?" Zane said as he pulled up to the house.

"Yes." She didn't turn to look at his features, already knowing what she would see. The square jaw, the brown hair, the day's worth of stubble on his cheek. Confidence that bordered on arrogance.

And complete disinterest in her.

It made her wish she could feel the same way about him. But just riding in the pickup with him had spun her stomach like a cotton candy machine, and she couldn't stop breathing in his scent. It reminded her of cut grass and hard work. It smelled good and right, and it wouldn't be hard to get addicted to it.

Yeah. This might have been a *very* bad idea.

How could she be a mother to their children if she was an emotional mess because the man she was married to didn't return a single one of the feelings she had for him?

She needed to be very, very careful.

The pickup pulled to a stop. She opened her door and hopped out.

There were two suitcases, and he could get them both, so she grabbed her purse and a small bag that she'd put behind her seat and started walking toward the back door.

Several little bodies went rushing past her, and she recognized Luke and John, followed closely by who she thought at first was Ophelia but then realized it wasn't. Too small for Cordelia. That was odd.

She'd spoken with Mrs. Hudson before she left, and Waverley had thought she might have brought one or two of Zane's nieces along to play with the children. That must be it.

Waverley stopped trying to figure it out in her head. There was an extra kid here, but with eight children, it really wouldn't matter.

She owed Mrs. Hudson a huge thank you. Not everyone was brave enough to watch eight kids at once.

"Hey, Mama! Mrs. Hudson said we were all to come in whenever you got back, so we could greet you and Mr. Zane," John shouted as he went flying by her into the house.

"I'm glad to see you're all obeying," Waverley said. There should be something better to call him than Mr. Zane. But she didn't know what. She wouldn't expect her children to call him "Dad" just because she married him.

Maybe she could give them that option. Some of the boys might decide to. John was serious but also pretty cuddly. And Roman might do it as well. The older boys would take some time, probably.

She walked in, followed by a couple more kids, and behind her, she heard the heavier footsteps of Zane. But she didn't turn around. Instead, she went to Mrs. Hudson.

"Thank you so much. I know it's not easy to watch eight children."

She had her arms out and was getting ready to return Mrs. Hudson's hug when, from behind her, Zane said, "Eight? You mean seven, right?"

"No, eight."

"Ten," Mrs. Hudson said.

"Wait. What?" Zane said, his voice holding an edge of panic.

"Ten?" Waverley tilted her head, feeling like her center of gravity had shifted, and she wavered.

Mrs. Hudson's blue eyes sparkled. "This might be a sign that your father could possibly be right, and you might be marrying in haste, just a little, if you don't even know how many children you have between you."

She emphasized each word of that last part.

"Mom. We've been through this. I'm old enough to make a responsible decision, and so is Waverley. And we did. We're also *not* doubting how many children we have between us. Seven."

"No," Waverley said, hating to disagree with him in front of his mother but knowing for a fact that he was wrong. "We have eight."

She turned, and their eyes met across the table. She was sure and held his gaze with confidence. His eyes were slightly narrowed and so blue they almost looked black. Thoughts ran through them as he tried to figure out why they weren't in agreement on the number. It wasn't like a kid just dropped down from the sky. A person had at least nine months' notice, and all of their children were in school. So that meant a half a decade or more on this earth.

On her right, Mrs. Hudson shifted and maybe bit back a smile, but his mother was wise and kept her mouth shut.

This was probably something they should have figured out on their own.

"I have four girls. And you have three boys," Zane said slowly.

With each sentence, he held up a hand with the proper number of fingers on it. "That makes seven," he said in the same slow voice.

If his words hadn't shocked her so much, Waverley might have interrupted him. But as it was, she stood staring at him with her mouth open.

He had four girls? But she'd only seen two. There'd only been two in the restroom.

Even as she thought that, it was obvious that someone else had been watching the other two that night. He just hadn't mentioned that. Or maybe they were staying home by themselves as her boys were. And obviously, the thought struck her now, he hadn't realized that she didn't have all of her children.

How had she not told him that? How had she not mentioned that she had six kids?

"Okay. I see where the discrepancy is. And..." She swallowed, knowing that this would not make him angry but would probably shock him as much as it had just shocked her. "You have four girls, and I didn't know that. I thought you had two."

She tried to smile. She figured it probably looked more like a grimace, because his face tightened, and he was obviously waiting for her next words.

"And I...I had three boys with me the night that we were stuck in the bathroom at the truck stop." She said it slowly and lightly, as though saying it slower would somehow ease the shock of what she was about to say. "But apparently I never mentioned that I had left three of my boys at home....for a total of six boys."

Yeah. Definitely the man was surprised. His mouth opened and closed a few times, and so did his hands hanging over the handles of the suitcases that were sitting on the floor on either side of him. He also blinked like a two-by-four had suddenly landed in his eye. Or both eyes.

"That makes ten kids," he said fatalistically. The way any normal person would say such a sentence when they just realized that they now had a family of ten kids.

Normal people didn't have ten children in their family.

Waverley sighed. She had never really been in the ranks of normal people. But this made it official. "Yes. Six boys and four girls." She watched his face as she said it, wondering if this would have changed anything about the last three days if he'd known.

She doubted it. But ten seemed like so much more than seven.

Ten seemed like so much more than the eight that she had figured.

Ten.

Wow.

"Well." Mrs. Hudson dusted her hands off and then brushed them down her front. "I'm so glad we got that straightened out."

There was definitely humor in her voice. Waverley supposed that was a good thing. If Zane's mother could find this funny, she ought to be able to find it funny too.

If there was anything that living with Dexter had taught her, raising six boys on her own, it was that if a person had the opportunity to laugh, they should never pass it up.

So she laughed.

Until a thought struck her. "You did see that we brought two dogs with us, correct?" she asked, her laughter fading abruptly.

"No. I wonder how they got along with my two dogs."

Mrs. Hudson, bless her, doubled over into laughter. Between chortles, she said, "I think this is about the funniest thing I've ever witnessed. I sure wish I'd be around for your fiftieth wedding anniversary. I would love to tell the story to your grandchildren." She sobered long enough to look between the two of them. "Cats?"

Waverley shook her head.

"Just barn cats. And cows. I have a lot of cows." His eyes looked Waverley up and down. "But that's not a surprise to anyone, right?"

Waverley laughed. "No. That's not a surprise."

"As much as I would love to stay here and find out what else you two don't know about each other, I need to get going." Mrs. Hudson put her arms around Waverley and squeezed, an apple pie-scented hug that felt like home.

Waverley didn't want to let go. Her own mother's hugs had been very clinical. The three times she could remember getting one.

"Welcome to the family, sweetheart. I think you're going to fit in just fine." She nodded as she said it, then patted Waverley on the shoulder as her hands dropped away. She walked around the table and put her arms around her son, reaching up as he bent over.

"You got a good one this time, honey. I think you need to make sure you take care of her."

Zane's eyes lifted. Waverley didn't look away soon enough, and their gazes met and held. "Think you're right, Mom. I'll try."

He still wasn't smiling; she thought he might still be a little upset about the dogs, too. But it just wasn't something that she'd thought to mention when they were sitting on the floor in the bathroom.

And to be fair, he hadn't either.

# Chapter Seven

The chaos in the kitchen continued around him. Kids and dogs, running and yelling and barking.

His mother continued to hug him.

But somehow Zane's world narrowed, and all he saw was the woman standing across from him, meeting his gaze.

Tall and straight, her shoulders back, her chin up, and her gray-green eyes level.

He'd just pledged his life to that woman. Kind of unbelievable. But as the noise faded around them, and his mother slipped away with a few words that he nodded at but didn't really hear, he knew he'd made a good decision.

Had he ever looked at her before? Really looked at her?

He'd thought she wasn't classically beautiful, not like Vicki had been. But there was something that radiated out from her. Something warm and honest and strong.

Character. He could see character when he looked at her. Somehow it didn't matter that her chin might not be the perfect angle or her eyes weren't set just so. What he saw shining out from inside was more valuable, more desirable, than any outside beauty.

It attracted him.

Which scared him.

He didn't want to be attracted to his wife.

Friends, yes. Coparents, definitely. Partners, maybe. Lovers, eventually.

But he wasn't falling in love. He wouldn't. He'd done that once and felt nothing but regret over it. Never again.

So, this attraction, this pull toward her, this odd desire to just stare into her eyes needed to be dealt with, and immediately.

He ripped his eyes away.

Looking around, he saw his mother had already left, and there were kids and animals everywhere.

He supposed he might as well get used to it. This was going to be his life.

However, he could get used to it in stages.

"Let's put the dogs outside for now." He looked back over at the woman who hadn't moved, staring at her forehead rather than meeting her eyes. "Will your dogs stay around?"

The forehead wrinkled. "Probably."

"I'm not worried about them going to the neighbor's property, unless they're prone to running off. We own everything we can see from here. I just don't want to lose them."

"I don't think that will happen. But we did live in town, and they've never been able to run loose before."

"We'll watch them then. They seem to get along okay with my dogs."

She nodded, her eyes scanning the room as their kids grabbed the dogs and put them outside.

He took a breath. He hadn't realized he was taking responsibility for six more kids. He glanced around again. All boys, like she said. His heart smiled a little because he loved his girls but he'd always wanted boys, too.

Girls could drive and work just as well as boys, better in some ways, but often they weren't as interested in that direction. Even now,

Cordelia, at twelve, stuck out her lip when he asked her to come out with him. Maybe that was just the attitude she had because she didn't want to be with him.

He couldn't think about it.

"Okay, guys. I think we need to introduce ourselves." Most people probably did that before the wedding. He almost laughed at the thought.

"I want you to line up, and we'll say our names, so that..." His eyes skittered over to Waverley. What should he call her?

They hadn't talked about this.

He decided to make it up. "Miss Waverley and I can learn them all."

His eyes skittered down the line of his girls. They had a mom, and he wouldn't expect them to call Waverley "Mother" or any variation thereof.

But they could have the option. "You can call her Mom, Mom Waverley, Miss Waverley. Any of those work. As long as you're respectful."

His girls blinked up at him with big blue eyes, except for Cordelia's brown ones. They were a little narrowed, like she was annoyed at him for even suggesting that they might use the word "mom" for Waverley.

She could just get used to it. One thing he was sure of, he and Waverley needed to be on the same side. Whatever side that was. They needed to stand together.

Hopefully she would back him on this. Maybe, at some point, he'd start to get ahead of things, and they could talk about them before they came up with the kids.

"As for you boys, you can call me Dad if you want to. Or Mr. Zane. Or any combination of Dad and Zane; again, as long as it's respectful."

Okay, blending a family was a little more complicated than what he'd pictured.

The kids had kind of ambled over, and all stood in two loose groups. Boys in one group, girls in the other. Would that be the way it always was? His kids and her kids? Was it too much to ask to be able to have them function as a family?

Was there something, or some things, that they could do to promote unity and make them a cohesive family unit?

Questions he never thought he'd need to answer. But he'd always longed for a strong family. Today, it almost looked like there were sides.

It probably didn't make it any easier that it looked like boys against girls, too.

It certainly didn't help that he didn't really know his girls much better than he knew Waverley's boys, and he definitely didn't have any confidence in knowing how to be a dad.

But other men had figured it out. He could too.

"Now..." He looked over at Waverley. Remembering to soften his tone, he said, "Would you like to come over here beside me? I'll introduce my girls to you."

He thought maybe he did okay, because her lips tilted just a little, her head angled, and she moved immediately to his side. Not close. Not touching. A foot away, but close enough that he caught the deep scent of vanilla and laughter, cinnamon and moonlight, that he'd noticed in the pickup and also at the church. It was a good smell. Wholesome and clean, and completely natural.

He resisted the urge to put his hand on her back. It was the first time he felt compelled to touch her, and it was weird to have to fight that.

She was his wife. Why should he?

So he didn't. His hand landed between her shoulder blades, with his thumb on one side of her neck and his fingers on the other.

He thought of her as sturdy and strong, but under his fingers, her neck felt slender, almost delicate.

Her long hair was up. He hadn't seen it completely down, but he guessed it would fall down her back somewhere. Wispy strands flirted softly over his hardened knuckles, and he had the oddest desire to move his fingers up and down over the soft skin under them.

He shook his head. He was introducing his girls. He wasn't supposed to be distracted by touching his wife.

"You know Cordelia, she's twelve. You also met Ophelia, who's five." He indicated the girl standing closest to the boys with a smile on her face. "That's Juliet, and she loves jokes. She's eight. And lastly there's Beatrice. She's seven."

His fingers squeezed her neck, and he almost thought she suppressed a shiver. But maybe that was just his imagination. Definitely the little hairs that were whispering over the backs of his fingers made *him* want to shiver.

"Nobody expects you to remember them all with just one introduction. And, girls, maybe you can help her if she forgets?"

"I think I'll remember. I recognize all the names from Shakespeare." Waverley lifted a brow and tilted her head at the girls as though asking if she were right.

Zane was about to answer for them, but Juliet giggled. "Mom said there weren't any hicks in this town that would know any Shakespeare."

Again, Zane opened his mouth to correct his daughter, but Waverley beat him to it.

She laughed. "Maybe you can help me, because my Shakespeare is a little rusty. I read some in school, and I really loved it. But I haven't read any for a long time."

"My name is from *Romeo and Juliet*, of course. Only I die." Juliet seemed to think that was very funny, and she snickered, putting her hand up in front of her face like maybe she knew she shouldn't snicker about her dying.

"I think I remember that. Romeo dies too, doesn't he?"

Juliet nodded, still snickering.

"Do you want to introduce your boys?" Zane asked. He kinda liked the way the conversation was going, but the boys were getting restless, and so was he. He had a lot of work to do, and he'd been spending a lot of time going to the lawyer and setting up paperwork.

She stiffened a little under his hand, like maybe she resented the fact that he was pushing to get this done quickly.

Maybe she was right. Not five minutes ago, he'd thought to himself that he wanted to have a cohesive family, and yet here he was, anxious to get through the introduction so he could go out and do the work that was calling to him.

Waverley spoke. "I think it would be easier, boys, if you lined up in order."

She didn't raise her voice, and it didn't come out like a command, but immediately the boys started moving around. There was a little bit of pushing and shoving, and a couple boys stumbled, as they figured out where they belonged in the line. As soon as they settled down, she began.

"Matthew, thirteen. Mark, eleven. Then Luke who's nine. Those are the ones that weren't in the restroom. They were home cleaning up the kitchen, and then they went and helped your brother dig up the septic line at the church."

She turned her head to look at him, and he looked down, which was a mistake. Because her eyes caught his again, and they seemed to be saying more than what he heard coming out of her mouth. Maybe there was some admiration there. Maybe that attracted him.

Maybe she saw admiration shining back at her, because her children were well behaved. He'd been a boy at one time; he knew how hard it could be to get little fellows to listen. Not to mention her life had just changed, completely and irrevocably, and yet she was calm and seemed to be completely at peace.

Then there was that glow he'd seen earlier.

He shoved those thoughts aside and moved his eyes away, back to the boys. "I think I see the pattern. New Testament books. The first five?" He thought for a second. "Acts?"

"Yes, only we spell it 'A' 'X,' and he's six. And before him, there's John, who's eight."

The little boy smiled, a dimple popping in his cheek, his hands behind his back. He moved his body back and forth, although his feet stayed planted on the ground, like he just couldn't stand still.

Zane totally understood that feeling. He'd felt that every Sunday morning sitting in church, swinging his legs under the pew, keeping his butt still on the seat. So hard for a little boy to be still. His mom had frowned on the swinging, but as long as his butt didn't move, he wasn't in trouble.

"And of course, there's Roman. He's five. Sounds like he's the same age as Ophelia, and he's in kindergarten this year. I believe they're in the same class."

He'd just registered his girls for school last week, and they seemed to be adjusting okay. He hadn't had a chance to figure out who was in their classes yet, though.

Cowboy Crossing wasn't a huge town. He thought there were just four kindergarten classes with twenty kids each or so.

"Okay, well, I have more names to learn than you do, but I think my names are easier."

She smiled up at him, an easy smile. There was no flirt in it, or coyness. It was just a real smile. He blinked a little, because he hadn't been expecting her to be beautiful when she smiled so close to him.

But she was.

His heart leapt in his chest, and his fingers, which had never left her neck, tightened.

Her eyes shifted just slightly, and something, almost alarm, maybe, because of the pressure he was exerting, entered them, and he realized immediately what he was doing.

He dropped his hand and stepped back, turning to the children.

He went through some ground rules, normal things, the rules he'd always had for going outside, mealtimes, and chores.

He ended by saying, "Miss Waverley and I will discuss some things and will decide how we're going to handle any issues that come up. But you respect her as an adult in this house, and you will listen to her as well as me."

Maybe he was a little commanding. He knew he had a tendency to be that way. But he wasn't going to pretend to be somebody he wasn't. And he definitely wasn't going to live in a house with ten kids, letting them run all over him. There had to be some order and discipline.

Thrusting his jaw out, determined that he would not get sidetracked by eyes or skin or wisps of hair that tickled his nerve endings and seemed to reach deeper where he definitely didn't want feelings to go, he looked at Waverley. "Do you have anything to add?"

"No. Not right now. We'll get settled for a few days, then we'll figure some things out."

He jerked his head. "Then if you don't mind, I've some work to do outside. If your older boys want to come, they're welcome. Cordelia?"

He wanted her with him; he'd missed so much time with her. But she shook her head.

"If you don't go with your dad, you could help me make supper."

Cordelia's eyes narrowed, like she thought she was going to go play if she didn't help her dad. But she jerked her chin up and set a mulish look on her face. "I'll stay."

# Chapter Eight

Waverley stood in the kitchen, feeling like she needed to pull a Susanna Wesley and stick her apron over her head and just pray.

She didn't have an apron though, and she had at least five sets of eyes that were staring at her and a couple more that were already spinning around like they were looking for the next mess to get into.

She knew what to do with those little-boy eyes, and she gave them jobs in the living room arranging the boxes of toys, blocks, and trucks that Zane's brothers had helped move last night and this morning.

His brothers had gotten everything they could out of her house, and the rest of it they were leaving for the next renter.

Earlier this week, Zane had paid her rent for the last two months, which Waverley appreciated, but it made her feel like she was already starting out behind. Not that she thought they should keep a running tab of who paid for what, but she wanted to make sure that she was pulling her share. This wasn't supposed to be an arrangement that only benefited her.

The new setting would keep the kids entertained for a bit.

Right now, she needed to get started on supper.

Her three older boys and Juliet had gone out with Zane. Beatrice and Ophelia played with John, Ax, and Roman in the living room.

That left Cordelia, staring at Waverley with her arms crossed over her chest and her foot tapping on the ground.

Waverley felt like it was a challenge.

Well, she wasn't sure whether she could meet that challenge or not, but she knew she probably wasn't going to do it the way Cordelia expected her to.

"Do you know what your dad's favorite dessert is?" Waverley asked, knowing Cordelia probably didn't.

"No. And I don't really care either." Cordelia's lips pushed out, and her eyebrows lifted ever so slightly like she knew she was being disrespectful and was challenging Waverley to do something about it.

"My late husband loved pie more than anything. Apple pie was his favorite. I made them so much I got to be pretty good at making them, but my favorite has always been something with chocolate in it." Waverley tilted her head and gave a conspiratorial smile. "You look like a chocolate girl."

A little bit of the belligerence faded off Cordelia's face. The word chocolate had a tendency to do that to women.

"I might be." Her lips didn't tilt up, but they lost some of their pout.

"Chocolate cake? Chocolate-covered fruit? Chocolate pudding? Chocolate cheesecake?" She said the last with a little lilt in her voice, like that was especially tempting.

Cordelia wasn't mean, probably just deceived, and her lips twitched. "I've never had chocolate cheesecake."

"It's the perfect pairing. Chocolate and cheesecake. Both are perfect foods, and when they're paired together, you get manna."

"Manna?"

"It's food that God made to feed the Israelites. I guess I always think since God made it, it must be the best ever. But probably, it was the best in nutritional value, since it fed that whole people for forty years."

"What is that, some kind of fairy tale?" Cordelia seemed interested despite herself, although her arms were still crossed.

"Nope. It's Bible."

"My mom said the Bible isn't true, because if God really loved us, he would have put women in charge."

"Well, he kinda did. We're in charge of raising the next generation. Whatever we raise our children to be is what the world's gonna come to. We're just leading from behind." She winked. Her roles and interests had never been something she had an issue with. She supposed if she had more of a commanding or forceful personality, her parents would never have been able to force her into a marriage with Dexter. It hadn't been pleasant, but she did end up with her boys, and now she was married to Zane.

She couldn't really be upset at the way things turned out.

She wasn't quite ready to say that God had worked everything out, though, since it seemed like he'd taken the back way when the direct route would have been a lot simpler and easier.

But she wouldn't be who she was now if she hadn't spent some time on the back roads.

It made her think of the Israelites wandering around in the desert for forty years. They wouldn't have been a mighty army with the character and drive they had if they'd gone straight from Egypt into battle.

Maybe they needed those forty years.

Maybe she needed those dozen years with Dexter.

A new and interesting thought, but she had a preteen girl standing in front of her. She wasn't going to teach her the whole Bible today nor change her character in five minutes, but they could make a dessert for tonight.

"So did we decide on chocolate cheesecake?" Waverley asked, looking around the kitchen and wondering if they had all the ingredients. Zane's brothers had been supposed to haul all her kitchen supplies from her house to here. If they had, someone had also put them away.

"You decided. I don't know how to make that."

When Waverley opened the fridge and saw all the cream cheese inside, she said, "By suppertime, you will."

Cordelia's brows drew down, as though she wasn't sure whether to believe her or maybe whether to believe she was actually going to get to make cheesecake.

"I'll let you in on a little secret." Waverley lowered her voice and leaned forward. "The batter is the best part."

Cordelia's look turned to part shock, part intrigue. "The batter?"

Waverley nodded, hoping her smile looked girly and conspiratorial. She had three older brothers from her parents' previous marriages, although they hadn't lived with them all the time. No sisters. She'd never been around girls.

But she was one, so that ought to account for something.

"You eat the batter?"

"Not too much. You'll get sick if you eat a lot of it. But cheesecake batter, cookie batter, cake batter...it's all super amazing. I don't know why anybody ever actually bakes anything." Waverley gave a light shrug of her shoulders and sighed a little dramatically. "If you'd like to help, I'd love to have you. I'll make supper, and you can make something yummy for after supper."

"Can I do it all myself?" Cordelia asked, taking two steps toward Waverley.

"Sure can. As long as you follow the directions I give you. I won't have time to do it if I'm making supper. How much do you think your dad eats anyway?" Waverley had a pretty good idea that he'd be hungry when he came in from working all day, but she thought Cordelia might feel good answering questions, and also, it might help her to start to care a little.

"I don't know. A lot." Her tone still wasn't loving or admiring, but it had lost a little bit of the belligerence that she'd had when she talked about her dad earlier.

"Your mom must have really pretty brown eyes, and you take after her," Waverley said as she looked in the cupboards, trying to figure out where the bowls and spoons were and where her mixer had been put away at. "It was awful nice of your uncles to move all this stuff. All I had to do was pack the kids' clothes. And boys don't have that many clothes."

"My mom has blue eyes." Cordelia came over and stood at Waverley's elbow.

Waverley stilled. Because Zane had blue eyes. Her comment about Cordelia's mother had been designed to put Cordelia at ease and to make casual conversation. Not to stir anything up.

That was a twist she hadn't seen coming. Cordelia wasn't Zane's child. Did he know that?

Definitely family drama that Waverley didn't want to have anything to do with. Not right now. Not until she'd established a foundation for her own family. Obviously, whether Zane knew it or not, he considered Cordelia his child. And he longed, if Waverley was reading him right, for Cordelia to love him and accept him.

Waverley might be able to help with that.

By suppertime, Cordelia's cheesecake was cooling on the counter, and she'd ended up helping Waverley with the meatloaf and scalloped potatoes and peas and carrots.

They were talking without any awkwardness, and Cordelia had even laughed some which Waverley had to consider a success.

While everything was cooking, they had gone upstairs and figured out the bedroom situation. Cordelia had helped her, almost happily, unpack clothes and organize dressers.

They'd even taken some time to go outside and walk around while the little kids had scampered through the yard.

As they sat down for supper, Waverley was definitely feeling the tiredness of a long, hard day.

Zane and the boys had come in, and thankfully, he had insisted that they remove their boots in the mudroom built for that purpose.

That would save her a lot of work, not having to clean up dirty boot prints every day, and she appreciated it.

Hopefully later she'd get a chance to thank him for the consideration.

She and Cordelia had used chairs and a couple of benches that they borrowed from a picnic table outside in order to set the table with enough places for twelve people. Zane sat at the head, and the kids piled in on either side.

Waverley sat opposite Zane, and somehow Roman and Ophelia had ended up on either side of her.

"This smells good," Zane said as he settled in his chair, over the clatter of the children as they realized they had six on one side and only four on the other. Luke moved around the table to sit down beside Beatrice.

"Thank you. Cordelia helped me. She also made dessert. She's kind of excited about it."

"Oh really? Dessert?" His brows lifted, and he gave his daughter a look that wiped the belligerence off her face. How could she not bask under the pride and curiosity that Zane showed?

"It's a surprise," she said, unable to dredge up the belligerence again but still not completely capitulating.

Progress at least, Waverley considered.

"Well then, if it's as good as this smells, I'll definitely be saving room." Zane looked at Cordelia just a few more seconds, and she seemed to bloom under his gaze, before his eyes turned to Waverley.

She wasn't sure exactly what she saw in them as he seemed to speak to her across the heads of the ten children at the table between them.

Maybe gratitude. Appreciation. Surprise even. Maybe he was surprised that she and Cordelia weren't fighting. Waverley couldn't say that didn't surprise her, herself. She hadn't been sure exactly how things were going to go.

She hadn't had an apron to put over her head and didn't have time for a long prayer, but surely anything good was because the Lord had helped. Later, after the children were asleep in bed, or maybe early tomorrow morning, she'd have time to be on her knees in gratefulness. Things could've been really ugly today, and they weren't.

She probably didn't deserve the look that Zane was giving her now, but she returned it, because she could hear her boys talking about the tractor tire they'd fixed, and the siding they'd put on the shed, and the spouting that they'd put back up, as well as something about hay and cows and the skid loader.

Her boys were going to love it here. Zane had been good with them.

The children quieted as Zane said the blessing and the food was passed.

The kids did a lot of talking about their day, and Waverley didn't say much. Maybe getting married was more stressful than she'd thought. Maybe that's why she was so tired.

The boys cleared the table while the girls washed the dishes, and it didn't take long to clean the kitchen while the kids went up to start on showers.

Zane was sitting at the table with some kind of cattle paper in front of him when the last of the boys came downstairs from their baths, and Waverley was just finishing sweeping the floor after getting the meat out for the next day and adding to the grocery list for next week.

The boys had carried her guitar into the room, because it had been their custom that after supper and baths, she read them a story and they sang together.

As the kids called her, "Mom, are we going to sing?" Zane looked up from his paper.

They hadn't had a chance to talk about anything. There were a lot of things she'd like to discuss. Things that she hadn't even thought about, like what they would do after supper.

She couldn't imagine he'd be upset that they would sing and read, but she kind of wanted to do something as a family if possible.

They would never become a family if they didn't do things as a family.

"This is something that we normally did after supper. Do you have a better idea?" She wanted to say she'd go along with whatever he suggested. But if he suggested sending the kids off to do their own thing while they went and did their own things, she probably wouldn't want to go along with that.

Although, dreams didn't often come true, and her dream of a big family that worked and played and sang together just might not be something she ever got.

"I don't think there is a better idea," he said as he closed the paper and pushed back away from the table. "Do you really play the guitar?"

"Yes." She actually wasn't too bad at it either. Although she didn't say that, because it wasn't like she was amazing or anything.

"That's handy. Do your boys play any instruments?"

"No. Some of them can pick up the guitar and play, but we only have one. So I play it."

He nodded, seeming to consider that. "When I was a kid, my mom had a guitar. I don't even know what happened to it. But I used to try to play. Never got good at it though."

"You have nice big hands. Sometimes it's a stretch for me to get the chords. The neck on a banjo is slightly smaller, and I think it would be a better fit for my fingers..." Her voice trailed off.

She did used to dream about playing the banjo. But there had never been money to buy one.

"Something tells me it takes more than big hands to be able to play well."

She lifted her shoulder. "Time and practice. The guitar is not hard."

She had started to move into the living room, feeling him follow her. But she stopped and turned a little, surprised to find him so close. His nearness was a little disconcerting. He was bigger than Dexter, but it wasn't really his size. It was more his confidence or maybe his intensity. There was just something there that made her very aware of his presence, of more than just him standing in front of her.

"I wanted to thank you for taking the boys with you. Thank you for showing them that they could help you. I...I know they can work, because they've helped me for years, but I'm just overwhelmed, and grateful, that they can be outside and doing the kind of work that they were doing today." She said things badly, but at least she'd said thank you to him.

"I guess I could say the same thing about Cordelia. The cheesecake was amazing. I'm pretty sure she didn't hop over the counter and do it herself."

"She did everything herself. I told her what to do, but she listened."

He nodded, not saying anything. His eyes watched her with that expression in them that she couldn't read, the one where she wasn't sure whether he was admiring her, or was surprised at her, or was wondering what he was doing with her.

"I was hoping we could put the kids to bed a little early tonight and I would have a chance to talk to you. Maybe now that we've actually met each other's children, we can figure some things out."

She nodded. "I think that's a good idea." Her lips felt dry, and her mouth wasn't much better. She touched her tongue to them, and his eyes dropped.

His face tightened, and heat seemed to flare in his gaze. It matched the spark that tripped in her stomach and warmed her chest. She thought his look had been intense before, but it became even more focused and made her breath hitch. Some small part of her brain told her she needed to back away, to turn, but she felt trapped, ensnared, and attracted.

All she wanted to do was move closer, put a hand on his chest, and feel his arms come around her.

Her foot started to move.

"Mommy? Mommy, are you coming in?" John asked from right beside her. She hadn't even heard him walk up to her. "Juliet and

Beatrice don't believe me when I said that we all sing together. They don't even know any of our songs."

She took a breath, shaky, and backed up, pulling her gaze away from Zane, blinking and breathing and trying to regain her equilibrium. She put a trembling hand on John's head. "We'll teach them. You didn't know the songs either when you were a baby."

"I'm not a baby anymore," he said, not back talking exactly, but in a tone that sounded a little offended that his mother might consider him any less than a full-fledged man.

"Of course you're not, darling. But if you had never heard the songs, you wouldn't know them. Juliet and Beatrice will learn them in no time."

By the time she was finished speaking, thankfully the tremble had left her voice, and she felt like she could walk without needing to grab a hold of the wall.

It was the way she'd always felt around Zane, only multiplied, because she was married to him now.

Disappointment, or maybe it was bitterness, settled in her chest though, because she knew he didn't feel the same.

There was nothing she could do about it.

# Chapter Nine

"**D**addy, I'm scared."

Zane stood in the doorway of the room where Beatrice and Ophelia had their beds. Originally when they came, he had expected to give every daughter her own bedroom. But they hadn't been comfortable sleeping alone, and so he had doubled them up, never dreaming that there would be six boys and their mother moving in about a week later.

Waverley had taken two bedrooms, from what he could tell, for her boys. Which left his bedroom and one spare bedroom.

"Scared of anything in particular?" he asked.

Beatrice'd had the same complaint every night. Normally he went and lay down beside her until she fell asleep.

Tonight, he'd wanted to talk to Waverley. It was their wedding night. But they'd only known each other three days. Well, they'd known each other a lot longer, but they'd only been talking to each other for three days.

He was fine with that; he didn't need a lot of talking.

He wouldn't say he had a feminine side to be in touch with, but there seemed to be some little voice in his head saying maybe she wouldn't be okay with the three short days they'd had.

Whether it was consideration, intuition, or some kind of fear he wasn't facing, he thought that it might be a good idea for one of them to take the guest room for a bit.

He'd wanted to say that much to her, but he hadn't had a chance. Looking down the hall, he didn't see her at the doorway to either of her boys' rooms. Looking the other way, there was no light on in his room, either.

"Daddy." Her voice held more panic and fear than the last time, and he quit looking for Waverley and walked back into the room.

This was just one of the many things he didn't know how to deal with. Should he tell her to just suck it up, that there was nothing to be afraid of? Should he continue to lie down with her every night? Should he stay with her for five minutes? Should he pray and then leave? Tell her that Jesus was here so there was nothing to fear? It seemed a little trite, and he didn't want to be uncompassionate or uncaring.

He padded over in stocking feet and lay down beside Beatrice. "You get much bigger, and I'm not gonna fit on this little bed."

Beatrice had just been a toddler when Vicki had left. She'd been pregnant with Ophelia. He'd changed plenty of diapers, but he didn't really know her.

Maybe that was her problem. Once she got more comfortable here, she'd be okay. He could afford to be patient. Just tonight had been...a little different.

"Then we can lie on the floor." The fear was gone. Funny, all it took was his presence beside her.

"I'm a little old to lie on the floor. I wake up too stiff to move," he said, not really expecting her to understand.

"Is Miss Waverley really staying?"

He wanted to say yes. The word was on the tip of his tongue. But he didn't know. "Maybe" seemed too...open-ended.

Honesty was probably the best course. "I don't know. I guess we'll find out. I just know for sure I'm staying."

Beatrice settled down even deeper into her covers, and he put his arm around her, stroking her hair.

"Maybe Mom will come back."

Man, he hoped not. He couldn't say that, though.

Even if Vicki did come back, it wasn't going to be like what Beatrice wanted, although how she even knew what she wanted, he wasn't sure. She wasn't old enough to remember when they were actually a family anyway.

"Didn't you like singing tonight? And the story that Miss Waverley told?"

"Yes. That was fun. When Mommy comes back, she can sing and tell us stories."

He managed not to snort. Vicki wasn't exactly the sing and tell stories kind of person, although she did have a nice singing voice.

"Has Mommy ever read you a story?" he asked, pretty sure what the answer was going to be.

"No. But she will, if we ask her to, won't she, Daddy?"

"I don't know. I don't think she's ever going to live here though." He knew she wasn't going to, but he wasn't sure how strict he could be.

"I want Mommy. I want her to be here. I'm scared without Mommy."

He didn't doubt it. Her voice trembled, and he was pretty sure she was close to crying.

He tucked her closer to him and said the only thing he could think of that might distract her from her fear. "Did I ever tell you about the time Uncle Chandler clobbered me with a baseball bat?"

As he suspected, she giggled. "No."

He settled down to tell the story, wishing he could have had an opportunity to talk to Waverley but knowing keeping his child from having a panic attack over not having her mother here was probably more important. He hoped Waverley understood.

ZANE HAD NEVER COME to bed last night. She thought they'd made a decision about what they were going to do, and either he didn't keep his end of it or he got sidetracked somewhere.

She hadn't checked in the spare bedroom, because she wasn't sure she wanted to open the door and find that that's what he'd done without even talking to her.

She tried not to let it eat at her. She'd been through much worse, and she wasn't quite sure exactly why she was upset, except it felt like one more rejection.

She put her hair up and dressed in clothes she'd be comfortable working in all day. She had kids that needed to be gotten up and ready for school, breakfast to make, an order of baked goods that she had to fulfill for a friend of Chandler's who was staying at Cowboy Crossing for a week, of course there was the never-ending pile of laundry, and more unpacking. She had enough to occupy her for the entire day and then some. She didn't need to borrow trouble by wondering why her husband had never come to bed last night.

She exited her room softly, not sure exactly what time the bus came to pick the kids up but figuring she had a little bit of time to go down and get some things like lunches and breakfast going before she came back up and started on the kids. It shouldn't be that much harder to get ten kids ready than it was to get six, especially since Zane's girls were all old enough to get themselves mostly ready.

She'd taken three steps down the shadowy gray hall when a dark figure appeared in a doorway, and she bit back a gasp.

Zane stepped into the hall, closing the door with a soft click behind him.

They stared at each other. She hoped there was no irritation in her gaze, nor hurt. Neither one of those two emotions were things she wanted to feel. She didn't want to show them either.

She stuck her chin out and forced herself to meet his gaze, not lowering her eyes and hurrying on like she wanted to. Avoiding problems had never gotten her anywhere.

But she didn't think it was her place to talk first, either. She'd done what they'd said they were going to do. He was the one who hadn't shown up.

She didn't have to wait too much longer.

"I wanted to talk to you. But Beatrice has been having some trouble going to sleep. She's scared, misses her mom. Every night. I should've anticipated it, but I wasn't really thinking about it."

"That's fine." She knew all about kids that were scared. Roman and Luke both had a tendency that way. But neither one of them had said anything last night. She thought they were pretty exhausted from all the new things they'd experienced.

He ran a hand through his hair, and if she had to guess, she'd say he was agitated. "We haven't known each other that long, and I was planning on sleeping in the guest room anyway. I should have told you. I'm sorry."

Dexter never apologized. So that was kind of new. "It's okay. I wasn't lying awake worrying about it."

She was lying awake worrying about other things. Like if she'd made a really bad decision, since her husband hated her so much he couldn't even bring himself to come to bed.

She lifted a shoulder. "Not a big deal."

"Was just going to give it some time."

She pressed her lips together, trying to feel like it wasn't a rejection again. Nothing she'd ever done had been right for Dexter. She hadn't thought that being with Zane would be the same way. Maybe it wasn't, but it felt like it.

"That's fine. You can let me know when you've had enough time."

It was childish, because maybe the conversation wasn't over, but she walked away, going to the stairs and heading down them. She had a busy morning.

She stopped on the third step and turned around.

Zane hadn't moved.

"What time does the bus come?"

"7:40."

"Thanks." Glad they could still be civil, even though he'd hurt her. Maybe he hadn't meant to. Probably he hadn't.

If she gave herself enough time and said the right things in her mind, she could pretend that her heart hadn't pinched and cracked, dispelling just a bit more of the little-girl dream that she still foolishly held close to her heart. That someday someone would want her just for her. Not for the house that she came with or her ability to cook, clean, keep the house, or raise kids. Just her.

# Chapter Ten

Z ane threw a sack of feed on the back of Reid's truck. It landed with a thump. He and Reid always split a feed delivery, since the larger delivery was cheaper.

"Don't you think this was kinda sudden?" Reid said, having just heard from Deacon, who was also there, that Zane had gotten married.

Zane was pretty sure Deacon hadn't come to visit but just to check on him. Maybe, knowing Deacon, he was making sure Zane was treating his wife okay.

He hefted up another fifty-pound sack of feed and put it on his shoulder. "No. I don't."

If there was anything he'd learned as the oldest of six boys, it was he could never show weakness. And never admit a mistake. Just because last week this time he couldn't have told anyone Waverley's name didn't mean that he was going to admit that his marriage was sudden and that that might not be the best way to start a future together.

"So you've been seeing her and just haven't mentioned it to anyone?" Reid grunted as he came beside Zane and hefted up his own feed sack.

"Is this the Inquisition or something? I mean, I can answer these questions if you really need me to, but I had never really thought that my romantic affairs were of that great of interest to you."

He was being rude, although his words were true. Why would Reid care who he was dating or getting married to?

Deacon slapped his feed sack down and looked across the truck bed at Zane. He might be the oldest, but Deacon commanded respect somehow. "We're your brothers. We love you, and we care about you." His eyes slanted to Reid as Reid slapped his bag down over the tailgate and braced his hands on the end of it. "But I think you're concerned about the wrong person." Deacon's gaze, serious and probing, went back to Zane. "How is Waverley doing?"

"If you're so concerned about her, go in the house and ask her yourself."

Why was he being so belligerent? Maybe because he didn't appreciate people sticking their noses in his business. Or maybe because he knew that, typically, women needed a little bit gentler treatment than what he'd dished out. They'd been married a week, and they'd spent less than five minutes alone—*if* one added up all the times they passed each other in the hall with no kids around.

Waverley had settled into the routine of getting the kids up, cooking breakfast and getting them off to school, cooking lunch for him and the hands, doing laundry and cleaning house and somehow finding time to get her baking done, as well as cooking supper and helping with schoolwork.

They'd been singing and telling stories in the evening together, and she looked exhausted.

She also never looked at him. Not after the first day. It made him sad, because he'd liked the way she looked at him with stars in her eyes, like she admired him, liked him, and wanted to be with him.

She'd gone from that to not even looking at him. He wondered if he'd imagined it to begin with.

Deacon hadn't moved. "I take it that's a no."

"A 'no' for what?"

"A 'no' for you haven't been treating your wife very well."

"The way I treat my wife isn't anyone's business except mine and hers."

"I didn't want to see the same thing happen to you and Waverley that happened to you and Vicki."

Zane slapped his hand down on the side of Reid's pickup and gripped it tight. His words came out soft and pinched. "Are you insinuating that Vicki leaving me was anyone's fault except for hers? Did you forget she was the one who cheated and left?"

"I'm not insinuating anything." Deacon never got angry, but he was never cowed by anyone else's anger, either. "I'm flat-out telling you, you neglected her. I'm not saying that makes anything that she did right, and I'm not saying she wouldn't have done it anyway. But she needed a little more from you than a few minutes in the evening after supper. You get so wrapped up in your work and the things that you're doing, bossing everyone around, and starting project after project, and you never come up for air. Or look around and see anyone has needs but you."

"That's not the slightest bit true. Every day after school from the time her boys get home until suppertime, I've had them out with me. If any of my girls want to come, they're with me, too. I'm not saying I'm perfect, but I'm trying hard to be a good dad. You're not seeing it." He hated that he had to explain himself to his brother, but he couldn't stand that Deacon had just said that he had any responsibility for the failure of his first marriage.

He could see that Deacon might have a point.

"I wasn't complaining about what you're doing as a dad. We have a great example in our own father. But did you ever notice how he treated Mom?"

The question hung in the air as Zane stared at Deacon. Reid hadn't moved, and Zane almost forgot about him as he sifted through his memories, remembering his dad driving the tractor and teaching him. Wire-tying a block of wood to the garden tractor so that he could reach the pedals to drive. Man, he wasn't sure he was even in school. He'd been young. His dad had been a great dad.

But as he thought about it, he knew Deacon was right. He'd never really considered his mother. Of course he loved her, of course he talked to her, but he'd never really thought about her and his dad and their relationship.

He supposed he'd just looked around and found a good-looking girl, struck up a conversation with her, and fancied himself in love. He hadn't thought about what it might take to build a relationship and keep it strong.

But thinking back, his dad always made sure that whatever he was doing, his mom was involved in it.

"Between us, we have ten kids. She doesn't have time to follow me around like a puppy dog on the farm."

"Mom never did that with Dad either." Deacon raised his brows.

"I'm running a farm here, I don't have time to baby anybody." Zane knew the words weren't the nicest, but he didn't know what else to say. He couldn't just let the farm go to pieces while he was at his wife's beck and call.

Deacon's mouth flattened, but he didn't say anything.

"Hey, I hate to interrupt this important conversation, but my feed's loaded, and I'm scooting out of here." Reid's voice held a bit of sarcasm as he dropped his hand from the truck and backed up.

"Do you need anybody to drive to the airport?" Zane wasn't even sure why he was asking. He didn't have time to drive Reid to the airport to switch his kids. He had twins, and his wife got the one twin for six months and he had the other for six months, and then they switched. He thought sometimes they did something different on Christmas and New Year's, but he wasn't real sure.

If anybody should have had a marriage that lasted, it should've been Reid, since he had married his high school sweetheart.

But maybe Reid had done the same thing he'd done.

"Nah. Thanks anyway. She's renting a car and coming out."

Deacon's brows shot up, and Zane almost smiled. It wasn't too often that Deacon got surprised. "She's coming here? Staying with you?"

"No. She has our class reunion she's planning, and I guess she has some plans with some friends. She rented a cabin down by the lake. I'm staying here."

"Your kids might actually be together for a bit?"

"I'm hoping so." Reid nodded. "Thanks for the help with the feed. I'll see you guys around." He slapped Zane on the shoulder as he walked by him. "Congratulations on the wedding." His stride slowed just a bit, and he said, almost as an afterthought, "It might not be a bad idea to listen to Deacon. Usually he knows what he's talking about. He was right about my marriage. But I didn't listen."

Zane didn't say anything, and Reid went and got in his truck. He and Deacon moved out of the way as Reid started it and drove off.

"I'm sorry. I was sticking my nose where it probably doesn't belong. I just know Waverley is a good woman, and I think she's exactly what you need. But I'm not so sure you are going to be what she needs." Normally Deacon was a pretty straight shooter, but he kicked the ground with his boot and seemed to find the dust cloud fascinating.

Zane supposed it was probably hard to give him advice or even talk to him. He did have a hard time admitting that he might be wrong. Still, he knew Deacon's heart was in the right place. Deacon would do anything for his brothers.

And, to be honest, he didn't really want to have another Vicki situation or divorce. Although, he honestly had trouble believing that anyone would stay anyway.

"I don't want to get too invested. I know it's just a matter of time until she walks, too. None of us have a good track record with women; they have a tendency to walk out on us."

"Maybe that's because we're stupid. And there's a fix for that," Deacon said.

Part of Zane wanted to be offended that his brother had just called him stupid. But part of him had to agree—maybe he was.

He hadn't spent a whole lot of time trying to figure out how to get a woman to stay. Just assumed it was impossible. He supposed when he started from a place of believing that it was going to end, that kind of doomed the relationship from the beginning.

Almost as though Deacon could read his mind, his brother said, "What if you just put your whole heart and soul into it. What if you tried? What do you have to lose?"

"It hurts a heckuva lot when your wife leaves you. I know you've never felt it, but it's like she takes half of you with her, literally half, and there's no anesthesia that would numb the pain, and it lasts for a really long time."

He'd never been that frank with anyone before. But it was true. He hadn't even been that invested in Vicki, in hindsight. Not the way his dad loved his mother.

But then maybe Deacon was onto something. Maybe that was what the problem was. He'd never let go and loved without reserve. He'd never allowed himself to be vulnerable, because that's just not the kind of guy he was. He didn't want to have to do that, not even to have a great marriage. It was too much risk.

"Waverley's a solid woman. You can bank on her. I know it's tough to trust, but I would put money on the fact that you can trust her. She's not gonna pull a Vicki on you."

They walked over to the pallet of feed, and Zane put a foot up on it, leaning his forearm on his knee. Maybe just to put some distance between himself and Deacon.

"I'm not saying that you have to go in and be vulnerable tonight. I'm just saying that I think you can have a really good marriage with Waverley, if *you* put a little effort into it."

"I have put effort into it," Zane said irritably. Irritated that Deacon would flat-out say that he hadn't.

"Not effort. You need to show a little of your soft side. With your girls and with your wife. It's what they need." Deacon brushed his hands down his legs, then turned toward his car. "I think that dude that knows Chandler, and is some kind of contemporary of Madeline,

87

some kind of cooking dude, was in town just raving about Waverley's baked goods. He got something from the diner that was hers. I wouldn't be surprised if he's out here visiting. I'm sure he's gonna order some things." Deacon started walking toward his car.

Zane's stomach felt like it was on a roller coaster. "Wait. What?"

Deacon stopped and looked over his shoulder. "You heard me."

"Some famous dude likes Waverley's cooking? That's what I heard." All the brothers knew that Chandler was just as likely to have friends that you could turn your TV set on and see as he was to have friends that nobody knew. Madeline, who was married to their brother Loyal, was the same way. Their family, and by extension Cowboy Crossing, wasn't exactly a stranger to famous people.

But Zane had never thought that someone famous would get mixed up with Waverley.

Vicki had been lured away, not by someone famous, but by someone who had money. That relationship hadn't worked, but that was why she'd left him.

Zane wasn't a wealthy man, although he wasn't poor either. But he was definitely not famous. He couldn't compete with someone like that.

"Relax, bro. Waverley is not going anywhere. I just thought I'd tell you what was going on in town." Deacon had completely stopped and turned around, his brows drawn together, his head lowered a little, as though trying to get Zane to meet his eyes.

"I don't care. She'll find someone better, she'll leave with him." He shrugged his shoulder. "That's exactly what I was saying before. No point in getting attached. They all leave."

"Then why in the world did you get married? And why in the world did you make vows to one another? Do you think that doesn't mean anything to her?"

"It didn't mean anything to Vicki. Everyone else in the family, except for you, has felt the sting and burn and hurt of having someone walk out. You don't get it, because you've not felt it."

Deacon's lips flattened. He couldn't argue that, although Zane knew he was probably being too rough on him, because Deacon had been hurt. Just not by fickle women.

"Look, bro, sorry. I'll try to...do better. What? Should I tell her her hair looks nice or something?"

Deacon's eyebrows shot up. There was silence in the yard. "Are you serious? You have no idea?"

Zane looked at his shoulder. "I know exactly how hot a brand needs to be in order to put a good mark on a steer. I know I can tag an ear and band a calf in twenty seconds. And I can look at a cow and tell you exactly when her baby's going to drop. But women? I have no clue." No point in trying to pretend he did.

"Google is your friend, bro. Use it."

# Chapter Eleven

Waverley moved around the big farmhouse kitchen, which was definitely a nice benefit of her marriage. It was so much nicer than the one she'd had in their rented house in town.

The bus had pulled away five minutes ago with all ten of their children on it. She had several hours' worth of baking to do, plus lunch and supper to get ready, laundry, and some more cleaning. She also hadn't checked her online orders yet.

It was going to be a busy day.

In the two weeks since she'd gotten married, she'd settled into a routine. That routine didn't include seeing her husband much at all. She knew farmers were usually busy in the spring, and it wasn't like she thought he was outside goofing off.

Plus, he took any of the kids that wanted to go outside when they got home from school, and they helped him until suppertime. Most of the time, all of her boys were out with him. She couldn't complain about that. She'd never dreamed she'd have a life like that for her kids, and she knew they were under the influence of a man of integrity. He would be teaching them not just how to do jobs but how to live a good life.

Still, there was that nagging disappointment that she hadn't quite gotten control over. She supposed it didn't matter whether one was thirty or one was fifteen; when a person liked someone who didn't like them back, it hurt.

God had been far better to her than she deserved, and she couldn't dwell or focus on that small hurt. She needed to be grateful and count her blessings.

It was with that thought that she rolled up her sleeves and got the flour and sugar out after she put a package of frozen hamburger in the microwave to thaw.

She was just thinking about how she would move some of Zane's things around in her bedroom, since he seemed to have taken over the guest room. She'd offered to sleep there, since all his things were already in his room, but he'd just said "no," and then one of the kids had interrupted them, and the subject seemed to be closed.

That seemed to be how their conversations went. They started talking, and one of the kids interrupted them.

She could move his stuff over and put some of her things on the dresser with the mirror. It would make the room feel more like hers.

Her head jerked up as the door to the mudroom opened, and Zane walked in.

Her eyes were probably wide with surprise, because he didn't usually come back in after leaving in the morning. Not until lunchtime when he brought the hired hands, Buck and Dwight, who were both widowers and retired.

She'd been surprised that first day, thinking that she and Zane would have lunch together where they could chat and get some things worked out without the kids around, but he'd brought both old men in, and there'd been a feed truck driver who'd come in as well.

That day, she hadn't eaten anything, because she hadn't planned on feeding more than two people, and yet there were five at her table.

She'd known for the next day and from then on.

There was always at least four for lunch, and she'd had up to ten when the neighbor had dropped by along with his wife and two older teen boys.

She tried to modulate her features, removing the shock, wondering what he could want, and putting a pleasant smile on her face.

Drat her stupid heart anyway for always kicking up when he walked in.

He stood just inside the door, twisting his hat in his hands. He'd taken his boots off, and she looked at his stocking feet. Maybe she was staring, but she was trying to figure out what was going on.

Had he told her about an appointment he had? Had she forgotten?

She was sure she hadn't. They hadn't talked so much that she would have anything to forget, honestly. Just stuff they needed to know for logistics on making a trip to town for groceries and a couple of minor issues the kids had at school as they settled in.

When he continued to stand there and didn't say anything, she almost felt like it was her job to start the conversation. It definitely felt like it the longer he stood there looking at her.

How could it be her job to speak? She didn't know what to say, anyway. She was doing exactly what she was expected to do. He was the one who wasn't in his place.

He shifted, and his body leaned toward the door, almost like he was going back out.

Would he really walk back out without saying anything?

Finally, he spoke. "I...I...I thought I'd come in and...see if there was anything that you needed me to do."

They'd only been married two weeks, but Zane had never sounded insecure or anything less than completely confident. He certainly had never stood with his hat in his hand, twisting it and waiting for her to call the shots.

"Did you fall down?" she asked, her eyes scanning his body, her stomach twisting.

Had he bumped his head? She couldn't see any blood. She held a measuring cup in her hand, but she set it down and walked around the table slowly, trying to figure out where he'd been hurt.

His brows creased, and he eyed her with suspicion. "No. Why?"

She stopped. "Are you asking if I need anything in town?"

"No. I told you we just go to town on Thursdays, unless for some kind of emergency. Why?" His hand stilled on his hat, and his eyes seemed to intensify as they looked at her. "Did you need something?"

She shook her head. "No. You just asked if I needed help. I was trying to figure out what you meant."

His face scrunched, like she was missing the obvious. The hand that held his hat waved around the kitchen, indicating the room. "I know you have a lot to do in here. I was checking to see if there was anything I could do to help."

He meant in the kitchen?

"You're not busy outside?" She didn't mean to make him feel like she didn't have things for him to do, but she just couldn't believe that he was in her kitchen to *help* her.

"Buck and Dwight are out there. I have some things I need to do this afternoon, and I thought..." His eyes dropped, and he was back to twisting his hat again. After he shifted his feet, he blew out a breath and jammed his hat back on his head. "Never mind. Forget it." He spun on his stocking foot and took a stride to the door.

"Wait!"

He froze but didn't turn.

She had no idea what was going on, but she was starting to get the impression that he had actually come into the kitchen, thinking he was going to help her with the housework this morning.

"Do you know how to brown hamburger?" she asked hesitantly, not sure she was right. But if he were actually reaching out—it seemed like that was what was going on—she didn't want to reject him. Not even on accident.

"I don't want to be in your way." He seemed to be talking to the door, but he hadn't left, so she felt there was still hope.

"You won't be. I just didn't understand. I didn't realize when you said 'help' you meant in here. I'm sorry."

He turned slowly. Maybe it was her tone. Maybe it was her apology. Maybe it was her admitting she didn't understand, but his eyes seemed to search her face like he was looking for the punchline.

There wasn't one.

She supposed this was where someone else might be coy or wink or even say something a little flirtatious, but that had never been her.

She could learn though.

Although Zane hardly seemed like the kind of man who would appreciate anything that wasn't the flat-out truth.

He took a step forward and hung his hat on the corner of one of the chairs. "I guess it's my fault. I didn't explain very well. I thought maybe I could help you this morning, and we could get your work done. Then maybe you could spend a little bit of time this afternoon with me. I have twenty acres on the south side of the far Henderson field that's started to go to head, and I was going to mow it. I thought maybe you could ride with me. If you want to."

Okay, Waverley knew she was standing there in the middle of the kitchen like a simpleton.

She could be wrong, but she thought maybe Zane had just asked her out on a date. Maybe.

Maybe he wanted to talk to her and thought that would be the best way. But he could talk to her in the kitchen.

She tried to push her girly dreams aside. She spent the last two weeks trying to convince herself that it was a very bad idea to fall in love with her husband. She'd be friends. And she wouldn't do more. She was just setting herself up for a miserable heartache.

Plus, she knew she wasn't exactly a catch. There was no way she could get herself to feel like it was a good idea to fall into his arms the first time he tossed her a bone.

So she tried to lift a shoulder, in what she hoped was a casual way, and hoped there was enough distance between them that he couldn't see her hand shaking or hear the thumping of her heart.

"That sounds like fun. I'd love to." Pleased with the calmness and maturity of her tone, she turned back toward the counter. "You can brown this hamburger." She pulled the package from the microwave. "And I'll figure what else you can do so that everything that I need to have done today will be done by dinnertime."

He moved over beside her. "Okay."

"George Freely, the Hollywood director that knows your brother Chandler, and I believe he also knows Madeline, is stopping in at one to pick up the batch of sweet rolls he ordered. After that, I'm free to leave." She handed the meat to him over the sink. He reached for it, but as she stopped talking, he seemed to freeze.

"That's the big-shot Hollywood dude?"

"I guess. I don't know." Like a mom of six kids had time to watch TV.

"My brother was telling me that he was going around town saying what a great cook you were."

Zane didn't look particularly happy about it, but she didn't think it was because he was jealous.

She almost snorted at the thought. Maybe he just didn't like the town talking about his family. Although he wasn't saying anything bad.

She wasn't going to apologize for it, so she wiggled the hamburger a little, and he finished reaching out for it.

"You can brown this on the stove, then put it in the crockpot." She gave him a few more instructions on the meal she was putting in the slow cooker for that evening before she turned back to the batch of dough that was rising on the back side of the counter.

# Chapter Twelve

Zane wouldn't have called himself a slow learner, but he was afraid he was more hindrance than help in the kitchen. He browned the meat okay, but when she gave him a bowl of bread dough and asked him if he would put it on the table and knead it, he was pretty sure she'd have been better off doing it herself.

He'd spent his share of time training people and knew the feeling—the feeling of thinking he'd just be better off if they would leave and he could do it himself. He watched carefully for irritation on her face, but he didn't see any.

Wisps of hair had fallen out of the braid that she'd put it in and floated down the back of her head, and her face held nothing but patience and an occasional smile.

He was always so focused on getting everything done he didn't think to smile while he worked, or hum, as Waverley was also doing.

Since Deacon had left, he'd been trying to think of what he could do, because Deacon had been right. He might not want to fall in love with his wife, but he needed to build some kind of relationship with her.

He didn't agree with Deacon at all that Vicki leaving was any part of his fault; he couldn't see how there could be any excuse for someone to profane their marriage vows. But he could see how it was important for two people who were going to be spending their lives together and building a family together to spend time together.

He'd finally gotten the bread dough going kind of well while Waverley had three or four things going on the stove, plus she was folding the basket of laundry that sat on the chair.

"You're pretty good at multitasking." He focused on one job at a time, finished it, then started another one.

"I think it's a requirement of being a woman. I've heard that multitasking doesn't actually help you get anything done faster, but I feel like I'm doing something and not just standing and waiting for those things to boil."

He nodded. She still kind of acted like she wasn't quite sure what was going on. Like she was suspicious of what he was doing. It didn't feel natural, but he decided he should try to talk to her about it.

"I guess you're probably wondering what I'm doing in here?"

"You said you wanted me to go with you this afternoon."

"Yeah. But Deacon was here last week, and he talked to me a little bit, and some of the things he said made sense."

"Oh." She put a neatly folded shirt on the pile on the table and turned back to the stove, grabbing a spoon and stirring something. "So you're in here because Deacon told you to be?"

He couldn't see her face, and her voice held what sounded like casual interest. But maybe it was the slight tilting of her shoulders that made him feel like his words had hurt her.

Glad his position at the table allowed him to face her, he thought maybe it would be a good idea for him to try to figure her out. Deacon hadn't said that, but surely there were things that he could discover about his wife.

Interesting, because he had never thought about discovering anything about anyone before.

He didn't stop to question that but said, "No. Deacon didn't tell me to come in the house and work. He said that Vicki leaving might not have been all Vicki's fault. That made me angry, but it also made me think."

She nodded, her back still to him, as she picked up another spoon and stirred a different pot while adjusting the heat with her other hand.

"I thought...maybe we could be friends. I thought maybe we could like each other." There. That was being pretty blunt.

"Well, you don't have to worry about that. I've always liked you." Again, her words were superficial, and she seemed to be deliberately keeping them light.

He remembered the painful meeting they'd had before she'd married Dexter.

"Are you mad at me because of what happened when you asked me to marry you and I said no?" Could that be the cause of whatever wall seemed to be between them?

"No. That was a long time ago. I've not forgotten about it, of course. But I've changed from that person. I mean, come on, what I was asking was ridiculous. You'd have been a fool to say yes."

Those words at least sounded true. Her back was to him, and he couldn't see her face. Her body seemed stiff.

"I guess it doesn't matter anymore, but I'm sorry. I think I already said I made a bad decision that day."

"You did. It doesn't matter. Water under the bridge." She lifted a shoulder as she turned around, her face pleasantly bland.

Where had the admiration that had been on her face up until the day they got married gone?

That was a question he'd like to ask.

But those words wouldn't come.

He tried to think of courting words, words that a man might say to a woman as they were getting to know each other in a romantic relationship.

Deacon had suggested Google. He probably should have listened.

"If you could have anything in the world, what would it be?" He didn't know where that question came from. But he found he was truly curious to know the answer.

Her hands paused in the middle of creasing a shirt in half, and her eyes flew to his, as though wondering what had prompted him to ask. Or maybe whether it was safe to answer.

He knew he wasn't getting the deep answer when her lips curved in a little smile, just as pleasant and bland as the rest of her facial expressions had been, and she said, "I have everything I could ever want right here. Thank you."

"Come on, there has to be something."

"What about you? If you could have anything you ever wanted, what would it be?" She gave him a little smile, like she knew he wouldn't want to answer that question any more than she did, and put the folded shirt down on the table, grabbing a pair of pants from the basket.

His pants.

There hadn't even been a question about whether or not she was going to do his laundry. She'd taken that job on without him even saying anything.

"I guess I ought to thank you. Those are my clothes you're folding."

"Oh, you don't have to thank me. Not for the washing and the drying and the folding and putting away." She kinda tilted her head and set his pants down on the table. "But for any ironing, you definitely owe me."

He huffed out a breath. "I'll keep that in mind. I'll pay one of the girls to do the ironing."

Her face twitched, almost as though she wasn't sure how she felt about paying kids for chores, and he knew that was something that they needed to talk about, but he kinda felt like more than that, they needed a bond between them.

With this teasing, and a smile, something had tugged at his heart a little. He thought maybe she was loosening up some too.

But he wasn't really a teasing kind of man. He racked his brain for something funny to say and couldn't think of a thing.

"You didn't tell me that you were gonna have to marry Dexter, back when you asked me to marry you." It was the sorest subject in the room. Of course, he couldn't find anything funny to talk about, so he apparently just talked about the most awkward thing he could think of. He wanted to pat himself on the back or smack himself up alongside the head.

"It didn't seem to apply," she said while stacking another pair of pants on the table and turning back to the stove.

Whatever she was making smelled delicious.

"I assume you didn't want to, and I'm guessing your parents pushed you into it. Why didn't you just walk out?"

She answered easily with the same unemotional, superficial tone she'd been using. "I hadn't been raised that way. It seems like an easy thing for someone who was raised to be independent. But I never was. When he came around showing interest, I wasn't really interested, but I didn't fight whatever he wanted, and my parents encouraged me to allow it. I didn't realize how serious he was getting until he asked Dad if he could marry me."

She'd been stirring on the stove, and her hand stilled. "When I told my dad I didn't want to, he said that he and Mom were moving to a retirement community out east and that I couldn't come with them."

She swallowed. "I wasn't ready to be on my own. I had no idea how to survive. I'd done nothing but care for my parents and do what they wanted me to do. I know that sounds crazy, but it's true. I guess I'm a little ashamed to admit it now. But I didn't even have a driver's license. No money, and no other prospects. Seems ridiculous that I would even have gone to you but..." Her voice trailed off, and she turned her back completely toward him. Although he couldn't see her doing anything in particular at the stove.

"But what?" he prompted. Why had she chosen him? That was a question that had become more pronounced since their marriage.

He'd wondered at the time, just in a passing way, but now he actually cared about the answer.

"No reason."

It wasn't even close to being true. He decided to call her on it. "I think marriages ought to be based on honesty."

She spun, her eyes wide, her mouth open, but no words came out.

Her cheeks had gotten red, and she was holding a wooden spoon that dripped on the floor.

She stood like that for a moment, like she was getting ready to tell him off.

But she didn't, and her eyes dropped.

He could almost see as the anger deflated out of her, and she said, "You're right. A marriage should be based on honesty. Among other things." Her mouth closed, and she looked at the spoon before spinning back around.

"So you can be honest with me about why you chose me?"

"Maybe that's something I don't want to talk about."

"I don't figure a marriage should have secrets either." He didn't know where that line came from. He'd never actually thought about what a marriage should or shouldn't have. But no secrets seemed reasonable. Along with honesty.

She turned back around. This time, there was no spoon in her hand, but she crossed her arms over her chest. "It hardly seems fair that you're pushing me to spill any secrets I have while you haven't shared." She lifted her chin, the pleasant expression still on her face, but there was steel there too. It reminded him that she was no longer the helpless girl who had been abandoned by her parents and who had begged him to marry her.

The decision to get married was a mutually beneficial one. He'd needed her as much as she needed him.

"Maybe my secrets would scare you." He could think of a couple of things he could tell her that she didn't know, things he wasn't comfortable saying out loud. And yeah, he could understand why maybe she didn't want to share her secrets, because he wasn't sure he wanted to be quite that vulnerable either.

Had Deacon said he needed to be vulnerable?

He didn't think so, but he was pretty sure Deacon had said that he could trust Waverley. Deacon hadn't needed to tell him. He knew it. Had known.

It was just that he'd been burned, and he was...afraid.

It didn't sit well for him to admit to the fear.

"You tell me why, and I'll share something too."

"Ladies first?"

"I think the bread's done." He wasn't changing the subject. He wanted to be closer. Somehow it seemed easier to say the hard thing softer, and he was standing too far away from her. He picked up the glob of dough and carried it around the table. "You don't need to go first," he said. "I will."

She took the dough and put it in the pan she had prepared for it.

He put a hand on her shoulder. He could feel her bones, and his hand completely covered it. She was thinner than she looked.

She jerked a little when he touched her, and her eyes flew up, but they landed on his neck and stuck there.

His voice came out low. "My secret is I'm sleeping in the guest bedroom, but I don't want to."

Maybe if he hadn't been watching, he'd have missed the way her pulse jumped in her throat and the hitching of her breath.

All good things.

She opened her mouth, but he spoke before she could. "Now, tell me, why did you choose me?"

He didn't want her to comment on his secret. He didn't want to hear her say that he could keep staying in the guest bedroom. He also wasn't sure he was ready to hear her say, "you don't have to stay in the guest bedroom."

He knew what he wanted, but he wasn't sure what he was ready for. He wasn't sure what she was ready for, either.

She took two more breaths, her chest moving in and out, almost as though she were gathering her nerve, and then her eyes slowly moved up until they met his.

"Because you were the one I wanted."

"What do you mean by that?" he asked softly, his heart jerking crazily, like a wild horse on a tether.

Her head shook just a little, and her shoulder moved under his hand. "Exactly what I said. I told you, I did everything my parents wanted me to, and I was content where I was, because I'd never given it a thought. Maybe I wasn't ready to get married, but anytime I thought about it, you were the only one I could picture that happening with." Her eyes looked away, although her chin stayed up. "You are the one I wanted."

It wasn't a confession of undying love. He wasn't entirely sure what it was, exactly.

"Thank you. Thank you for your honesty, and thank you for answering my question."

She tilted her head, acknowledging his gratitude. "I'd better check the stove."

They worked in silence for another hour, until lunch, which he helped her serve and clean up.

They were almost finished when there was a knock at the door. Waverley had wrapped up George's order and set it on the counter. She hurried to the door. "That's probably Mr. Freely. He's right on time."

Zane didn't say anything. Irritation, or something like it, took a hold of his chest. He'd never even met this George Freely person, and for some reason, he didn't like him. Which was odd, since he always liked everyone.

"Mr. Freely, please come in. I'm Waverley." Waverley held the door open, and as he stepped in, she shook his hand.

"I'm thrilled to meet you, Waverley. I can't believe I've tasted the best sweet rolls I've ever eaten in my entire life here in a small town in the middle of Missouri. Why have you been hiding?"

Waverley's cheeks reddened, and Zane clenched his fist. He was happy for his wife, happy that someone loved what she had done, but annoyed at the same time. Why had he never tasted her sweet rolls? And why was a stranger being so friendly? Wasn't he standing a little bit too close?

Emotions he'd never felt before pulled hotly in his chest, and he took his eyes off his wife to look at the floor for a minute. Was he jealous? Was that what this was? Why would he be jealous?

"Mr. Freely, this is my husband, Zane. He's Chandler's brother."

George walked forward with his hand out, a smile firm on his face. Zane forced his lips up. He was afraid his smile looked more like a grimace.

What was wrong with him?

He stepped back while Mr. Freely chatted a little, wondering why he was having such a hard time. He'd never struggled with anything like this before.

George paid Waverley, and she handed the wrapped container to him. "I put a card on the top, in case you want more. That's my website. I mail things, but these are best fresh. If you're ever in town again, you're always welcome to stop in."

"You can bet you'll be seeing me again." George nodded and winked. The silver at his temples flashed a little. He looked like a successful Hollywood type, with what looked like an expensively cut shirt, tailored pants, and some type of loafer that wouldn't last two seconds around the farm. They were probably quite stylish, and expensive, if Zane had to guess. Not that he knew much about men's clothes. He wore what was comfortable and durable, and he'd never worried about anything else.

Again, Waverley's cheeks pinkened, and she smiled sweetly. She didn't look at that man like she admired him, like he was anything more than a stranger she barely knew, which was how she'd been looking at Zane since the night of their marriage.

Maybe it wouldn't be so bad, if she still looked at him the way she had before that. How could he get that look back?

Men like George wouldn't matter, if he felt like Waverley only wanted him.

Maybe that was Vicki's doing. Knowing that he hadn't been enough. And not knowing what it was that he had or hadn't done that had driven her away or not kept her. He didn't even know which it was.

Maybe being in the kitchen with Waverley, trying to build something, was a complete waste of his time.

"Zane?" He startled and realized that Waverley had said his name several times.

"Huh?"

"Are you okay? You look angry."

"I'm not."

Her lips pressed together, but she changed the subject. "Thanks so much for your help this morning. As soon as I'm done with the lunch dishes, I can leave."

There were just two more things to wash, and he watched her walk to the sink, graceful, with enough sway in her hips that they drew him.

He was going to be miserable company if he didn't get himself straightened out.

"Maybe you'd rather take a nap. I can work myself, and you can have the afternoon off."

She stiffened, and he might have missed it, except his eyes had been tracking her across the kitchen, and they'd stayed on her as she stopped at the sink.

"Whatever you want," she said.

He'd said that a marriage should be built on honesty, with no secrets between them. He supposed he should hold up his end. "I want you with me."

"Then I'll be there." She pulled the drain out. And turned. "Those last two things can wait. I'm ready now."

# Chapter Thirteen

"Okay, boys. One of you take this tractor back to the barn and the other can drive me out to the north forty where the skid loader is. We were loading chicken litter to spread on the fields this morning, and I want to bring it back to the shed." Zane pulled his gloves off his hands and shoved them in his back pocket as he walked away from the cows where they had just put a bale in the feeder, Matthew on one side of him and Mark on the other.

"I'll get the tractor," Matthew said. His chest puffed out a little bit, and Zane hid a smile. It'd been three weeks, and Matthew had gotten pretty good at running equipment. He was born to be in the seat.

Mark had a little more trouble. He reminded Zane of his brother Deacon. A little more introspective, a little wiser, but not as good hand-eye coordination. It had been harder for him to learn how to run equipment, but he was also more careful.

They were both good boys, hard workers, and willing to do anything he asked. He couldn't have asked for better.

He'd spoken with his parents and with Deacon again and found out a little more about Waverley's first husband.

He hadn't asked specifically, just listened to the comments they'd made. He felt like if he wanted to know about Waverley's husband, he should ask her. But when they'd mentioned him, Zane's ears had picked up.

The things he'd learned had made him appreciate her and the way she'd raised her boys even more.

"Okay, Matthew. Watch when you're taking it in the shed. Don't hit the sides of the door. Do it the way I showed you."

"Yes, sir." Matthew grinned and acted like he was going to run off, then seemed to get a hold of himself and strode away, tucking his own gloves in his back pocket exactly the way Zane had just tucked his.

It reminded Zane that more was caught than taught.

It also made Zane feel like he wasn't adequate for the job of raising ten kids.

God wouldn't have given them to him if God hadn't thought he was able.

*I need wisdom, Lord.*

Patience hadn't been something he'd struggled with. The boys listened well.

Mark and he walked to the four-wheeler, Mark swinging his arms along beside him and trying to match Zane's longer strides. It was odd, always having someone imitating him. A compliment, sure, but he wondered how long it would last.

"Cordelia thinks my mom really likes you. Are you guys going to stay together?" Mark's question came out of the blue. At least for Zane. He had his mind on tractors and chicken litter and soil tests and planting.

"I said I would. She said she would. I guess if we're people of our words, we'll be together 'til we die." He didn't know what else to say. He had his own doubts. But he could hardly voice them. Not to Mark.

"Cordelia thinks you need to be nicer to my mom."

"Huh?" Zane stopped and looked at Mark. He lifted his hat and scratched his head before settling it back down. "Cordelia said that?"

That was crazy. Three weeks ago, Cordelia looked like she was going to murder Waverley in her sleep. And now Cordelia thought that he wasn't being nice enough to her?

"Yeah." Mark stopped and swung around, childish unconcern in every line of his body. He had no idea how his one comment had stopped Zane's world. "She thinks you need to hold her hand and stuff like that. I told her that Mom never held Dad's hand, and Dad was a lot meaner to her than you are. She just doesn't know. She's got all those *ro-man-tic* ideas. The gross stuff girls always think of." Mark lifted his hat, just as Zane had done a minute ago, and ruffled his own hair before setting it back down. "Can I drive the skid loader back?"

"When we get there, you tell me how to run it, and if you're right, I'll let you." Zane threw a leg over the four-wheeler, and Mark settled down behind him. "You think about it until we get there."

And Zane would think about what Cordelia had said about Waverley. He supposed she was right. He tried to make time for her, at least once a week coming in in the morning and helping her with her stuff so she could spend the afternoon with him.

But mostly they ended up talking about the kids.

He felt like they knew each other a little better, and if they weren't great friends, at least they were friends. He thought she liked him okay, despite his flaws. Being too serious, being too focused on getting everything done that needed to be done, but how else was he supposed to run his farm, if he wasn't focused on the work that needed to get done? No one else was going to do it for him.

Thirty minutes later when they walked in the house, they immediately heard singing. That wasn't uncommon, nor was the laughter and yelling of the kids.

Luke had some kind of note sent home from the teacher about his homework not being correct, so he hadn't gone out with the boys, and

Zane thought Juliet and John had some kind of project to do, so they weren't out either.

But there was a lot of noise coming from the kitchen, so he doubted school projects were getting done. He tilted his head as he took off his boots. Was that "The Farmer in the Dell"?

He opened the door to see that they'd slid the table, completely set for supper, off to the side and put the chairs up in the middle. It looked like they were playing musical chairs, and Waverley was indeed singing "The Farmer in the Dell."

He wasn't sure what verse she was on, but when she looked up from chopping tomatoes and saw him, she immediately changed the verse and started singing, "The farmer's here for supper, the farmer's here for supper. Hi-ho the—" She stopped abruptly, and the kids scrambled for chairs.

Ax had been distracted by the opening door and with Zane and the boys walking in, and he wasn't prepared. He ended up with his butt on the floor, laughing.

"I'm out." He hopped up and ran over, wrapping his arms around Zane's waist.

That wasn't new, but it surprised him every time. He bent down, returning the hug, while silently thanking God that he was walking into a home full of love and laughter rather than one of contention and accusations like it had been when Vicki and he had been living together.

"Okay, kids, let's get the table back where it belongs, the chairs around it. This stuff is ready to be put on it, once you have it fixed in place." Waverley set food on the bar for the kids to carry to the table as they scattered to do what she asked.

It seemed like kids and dogs were running in every direction, but the table was being slid and chairs were being arranged, even though it was loud and boisterous and definitely more crazy than he'd ever thought he would come home to.

Still, it was friendly and welcoming and happy, and he realized with a start that he wouldn't want to be anywhere else.

He looked over the chaos at the woman who was arranging the tomatoes on top of the salad. Things would be a lot different if she hadn't said yes, if they hadn't gotten stuck in that bathroom together.

They were only a few weeks in, but she made him see that being a family could be fun. That home could be a place of light and laughter.

Did she really like him?

Maybe he should focus on Cordelia's other suggestion. That he could be nicer. It probably shouldn't matter whether she liked him or not. She'd thrown herself into doing the very best she could and making this work.

And he'd thrown himself into making the farm a success, feeling the burden of paying for not seven kids, but ten, plus a wife.

Of course, that was a major contribution to the family, and to Waverley, but maybe he should do more.

"Hey, Dad, did you have a good day?" Cordelia came over and kinda stopped in front of him.

She hadn't thrown her arms around him yet, but the day felt more likely now than it had three weeks ago. She'd definitely warmed toward him, and again, he probably had Waverley to thank for that, too, since Cordelia spent most of the time when she wasn't in school with Waverley. In just three weeks, she'd become a pretty good cook.

"I sure did, sweetie," he said, thinking that his day had become ten times better since she was actually smiling and talking to him and not grumbling and growling.

He opened his mouth to say more, but before he could, Beatrice screamed, "I hate spaghetti. My mom doesn't make me eat spaghetti. I hate it!"

Zane's head jerked up. He needed to take care of that.

Before he could do anything, Beatrice grabbed the big pot of spaghetti and jerked it toward the table, just as one of the dogs, Billy, ran through the kitchen, chasing Bambi, one of his dogs. Beatrice managed to stop for Bambi, but Billy plowed into her, and she was off balance enough that she and the entire pot of spaghetti went sprawling across the floor.

All the sound in the kitchen stopped except the echo through the house as the dogs ran through the living room and down the hall.

Beatrice sprawled on the floor, screaming in anger, but Zane didn't think she was really hurt, because she moved, pushing herself up, and her eyes narrowed, and her lip stuck out. She did slide a glance toward him, and he figured that was because she knew she was probably in trouble.

He hadn't quite figured out what to say before Waverley stepped out from behind the counter. "Does your mom prefer you eat spaghetti off the floor?"

Zane's eyes flew to her; was she serious? But immediately he saw the grin on her face and could hardly believe that she was laughing about the tomato sauce and noodles that were scattered everywhere.

Waverley must have felt his gaze on her, because she looked at him, laughter dancing across her face. She shrugged. Almost to say, what could they do about it?

He supposed having already had six boys, she was used to spills and messes.

The sound of the dogs grew louder, and Matthew strode over, grabbing Bambi's collar in one hand as she came out and snatching Billy with the other.

Beatrice, her lower lip trembling, pushed up. "No. She doesn't."

"Good. Then she and I have something in common, because I won't make you eat off the floor either." Waverley's voice was soft, and she bent her head some as though trying to catch Beatrice's eye.

Anger had been Zane's first reaction, and it still burned in his chest, although not as hot, because he could see the tear tracks on Beatrice's cheeks.

Waverley finished closing the gap between them, and when she touched Beatrice's arm, Beatrice started crying in earnest and turned and buried her head in Waverley's stomach.

"I'm sorry," she wailed. "I didn't know that the dogs were gonna trip me. I didn't mean to spill it everywhere. I'm sorry!"

Her voice was muffled because she spoke with her head still smashed into Waverley's stomach. Waverley stroked her hair with one hand while hugging her tight with the other.

"It's okay. The spaghetti mess is an easy fix, but maybe you can remember next time that we need to try to have a little better attitude, because a lot of times when we let ourselves yell and be angry, these are the kinds of things that happen."

Zane stopped. His mouth closed. He hadn't been going to let Beatrice get away with her disrespect and her bad attitude, but he kind of thought that Waverley had handled it well, and Beatrice had been "punished" by tripping and spilling supper all over the floor.

Matthew put the dogs out, and Mark, along with Juliet and Cordelia, had begun to clear up the mess by scooping the spaghetti noodles and putting them back in the pan.

"You guys aren't going to serve that, are you?" Zane said in a low voice, not wanting to interrupt Waverley and Beatrice but also not wanting the kids to have the mistaken idea that they were going to eat that after it had been on the floor.

"No. I just thought it would be easier to carry out if we had it in the pot," Matthew said.

Zane thought if it'd been up to him, he'd just let the dogs clean the floor themselves.

He was about to suggest they let them lick up the tomato sauce, if they would, when Waverley's voice floated over. "I made meatballs, and we'll just have meatball sandwiches instead of meatballs and spaghetti. It won't take any time at all."

He nodded at her. "Tell me where the rags are, and I'll wipe that after they're done getting the noodles cleaned up." He couldn't help but add, "Unless you want to let the dogs lick it up."

He didn't get the horrified look he'd been aiming for; instead, he got a lopsided smile. "How about you choose?"

"I'd rather let the dogs do it, but I think it might be more sanitary if I use a rag."

"I'm good with both choices," she said. "Anything that gets the mess off the floor."

He found a rag and wiped it up. As they were setting the food on the table, he took Beatrice into the living room and talked to her for a couple of minutes.

If she hadn't been truly contrite about what she'd done, he probably would have been stricter with her punishment, but he felt she'd been through enough. He also thought she'd probably get a little bit of ribbing from her siblings, because all the little ones loved spaghetti and were disappointed about the meatball sandwiches.

Supper proceeded without a hitch, but he hadn't forgotten what Mark had said, and so when they were finished, he pushed back away from the table.

"I'm going to take your mother for a walk. You kids can clear up the table and get the dishes done and the food put away." He said this without looking at Waverley. He didn't want to give her the chance to say no to him.

He wasn't quite sure why he was afraid that was going to happen. Maybe because Vicki had never seemed to want to do what he suggested.

Waverley had always put aside anything they hadn't gotten done to go with him in the afternoons. She'd never turned him down. Yet, anyway.

He stood. "Waverley, do you have anything in particular you want to give instructions for, before we go?"

He didn't look to see if she followed him as he walked to the door. If she didn't come, he'd be taking a walk by himself and looking like a fool in front of all ten of their kids. He supposed he was being an idiot.

He should've just said, "Waverley, would you like to go for a walk with me?" Why was that so hard?

He opened the door to the mudroom and walked out to put his

boots on. Before he closed it, he could hear Waverley's soft voice, and it sounded like she was handing out orders. He didn't relax until the mudroom door opened, and she slipped through.

She was going to come after all. There was relief in his chest but also...excitement? Anticipation maybe.

He found he actually wanted to take a walk with his wife.

# Chapter Fourteen

"I wasn't sure you were going to come," Zane said softly as he straightened the cuff around his boot and stood.

Waverley's silly heart beat harder, even though her feelings had been hurt by the brusque manner in which he'd "invited" or more like "commanded" her to take a walk with him.

On one hand, she wanted to smile a little, because it was so classic Zane—he was a commander through and through, and asking wasn't something that came easily to him. But, at the same time, it would have been nice if he could have said he wanted to take a walk with her, or something along those lines to let her know how he felt, rather than just throwing out a commanding announcement and expecting her to trot along behind him.

"You know you could've asked." She smoothed her hands down her pants and tilted her head to look at him. He hadn't turned the light in the small mudroom on, even though it was dusk outside.

Still, she could see his strong nose, the outline of his commanding chin, and the width of his shoulders, could feel the heat that radiated off him.

Of course she would want to walk with him. How could she not?

Especially when her boys came in every evening after working with him either after school or all day on Saturdays, smiling at him and acting more like men than boys every day. At mealtimes and bedtime, she could hear Zane in their speech now. Hear them discussing things he told them and things he taught. Hear the respect in their voices and their eagerness to please him.

There was no money that could buy that, and even if she didn't like the man, even if she weren't attracted to him, she would have to admire and respect him for that.

"I didn't want to give you the chance to say no." He opened the door and waited for her to go through, though what he had just said shocked her.

"What made you think I would say no?" she asked, trying to keep the incredulity out of her voice.

He closed the door behind her and followed her down the steps and out the walk.

"I thought we'd walk out toward the pond," he said.

She thought maybe he wasn't going to answer her question, but after a few steps, he said, "I know it's not fair to you, but sometimes I see Vicki, if not in you, in some of the things you do. Even if I don't see her, I remember what she's done, and I guess sometimes I think you're going to do the same. Sorry."

So basically, she triggered him, not by doing anything, just by being herself.

She wanted to sigh in frustration. "There's nothing I can do about that."

"No. It's just me needing to get over it, I guess. It's hard."

"I can kind of understand. I know you've had a long, hard fight."

"Vicki did a lot of lying. And I believed her at first. I even believed her later, because it's hard not to want to." The full moon was just peeking up over the horizon as dusk settled down around, and the peepers chirped loudly from down over the hill near the pond. A soft breeze blew and pushed strands of hair back away from her face. It felt good, like a gentle hand and a soft touch after a hard day.

The light was bright enough that she could see his jaw jutting out. In the little bit of time that she'd known him, she'd figured out that usually meant he was fighting not to feel.

"You don't have to tell me anything." She wanted to know everything. But she didn't want him to have to struggle through it when he didn't want to.

She wanted him to *want* to tell her. Not to have to.

"My brother said our divorce wasn't all Vicki. I thought about that long and hard, because I don't like to think that any of it was my fault. Looking back, I think she would have still lied, she still would have cheated, and she still would have left, but Deacon's right. I didn't spend a lot of time with her." He shoved a hand in his pocket and slowed, looking over at her. "I don't want to make that same mistake with you."

She slowed along with him, but she was grateful that he didn't stop. She didn't want to have this conversation face-to-face. It was easier to talk to her side and not have to look him in the eye.

The stone road was barely visible. She studied it as she spoke. "I don't want you to spend time with me because you feel like you have to. It doesn't really mean anything then." She blew out a breath, frustrated because she really wanted to walk with him, but she wanted to be honest. "I guess that's why you're coming in and helping some mornings, and taking me with you in the afternoon occasionally, because you feel like you *have* to spend time with me. It kinda sucks the joy right out of it." She risked a glance over, and he was staring down at her, some cold, dark, glowering look on his face. "Doesn't that make sense to you?"

"You said you didn't want to spend time with me."

She closed her eyes, grateful she didn't have to use them to see where they were going. The road was straight. "No. That's not what I said. I said I didn't want you to spend time with me because you feel like you have to. You know, one more thing for you to check off your list. Do you want to be a part of my to-do list?"

Zane lifted a shoulder, like it didn't matter. Maybe it didn't to him. "So it's not enough just to spend time with you? There have to be certain feelings attached to it?" He made a sound of frustration. "I can't pretend to feel something I don't."

Those were hard words. They made her shoulders want to fold in and cover her heart. "I would never want you to pretend to feel something that you don't. That wouldn't be honest. And I think we agreed that honesty was important."

"We did."

"Then I'm thankful you were honest."

They walked along in silence for a while, the moon slowly appearing above the mountain.

He spoke first. "I can tell you more about Vicki if you need me to. But I was kinda hoping you'd tell me something about Dexter. I've heard some rumors, but I thought if I wanted to know anything, instead of asking my family, who would probably tell me, I thought I'd just ask you." He hesitated. "They said he wasn't a very nice man."

"He wasn't." Somehow, talking about her late husband was easier than talking about the feelings that Zane didn't have. "He never hit the children, or even seemed like he might, or I would have left. But my parents gave him my grandmother's house when we got married. I don't know how he found out about the house and that my parents were giving it to me, but over the years, I've kinda figured out that was probably why he asked my dad if he could marry me."

He certainly had never acted like he couldn't live without her or like he was madly in love with her.

There weren't very many happy spots in her life with Dexter other than her six boys. "We ended up selling the house, because we needed the money. I'm not even sure what he spent it on. I never saw it." She hadn't even had the good sense to be upset about it. She'd had maybe three kids and been pregnant with the fourth or something. She couldn't even really remember. Those years just ran together.

After they'd sold her grandmother's house, they'd moved into the rented house. And she felt stuck.

"So it wasn't that he wasn't nice, he just couldn't handle money," Zane commented, casually, almost.

"I guess. He wasn't really interested in the children, and I did pretty much all the raising of them. It reminds me a little bit of you, not in a bad way, just that he just didn't spend time with us. Unlike you, he didn't have any character or integrity, and that's what I really admire in you."

There was nothing wrong with her telling him that she admired something in him even if he didn't return the sentiment. It didn't matter since it was the truth.

"I didn't know there was anything about me that you even liked, let alone admired."

The gravel crunched under their feet as they continued along the field road, and she wondered if maybe he needed that compliment. Maybe he needed others. Maybe, even though he seemed so strong and commanding, like he could stand alone through the winds of a hurricane, maybe having his wife cheat on him had made him insecure, and he covered it with things like the announcement that they were going for a walk rather than giving her the opportunity to reject him.

After all, Vicki had rejected him.

"I think everyone admires your good looks. Because you *are* very good-looking." Yeah. It had been a hunch, but when she said that, she could almost feel him grabbing her words and hanging on to them. Examining them. Wondering if she meant them.

"But I don't really think it matters what someone looks like. You can't really change that. You're born with whatever you're born with. It's the things that really matter that I admire so much in you." She paused, and she felt him tense, like he was waiting for her to speak again.

Her words probably wouldn't heal all those years of pain and rejection; it would have to be her actions, consistent over time, that would do that. But her words could start it.

"In the weeks we've been here, I've heard Matthew and Mark talking about you, talking like you, acting like you, saying the things that you say. Even when you're not around, I hear you in them, and it makes me appreciate you. I appreciate the things you're teaching them. Not just about farming. But I heard them talking about how a good man doesn't brag about himself but lets others do it for him, if he deserves it. I know they're too young to pick that up on their own from the Bible. I'm sure they heard it from you."

She kept talking. "There have been several other things too. Things that they've said that have shown me your character. I respect your integrity. And yes, I admire that in you."

They walked on, going up a little rise before the road dropped down and angled on a diagonal toward the pond. She could smell the earthy scent of the water and the pungent odor of rotting vegetation. This early in the spring, it wasn't bad, although as the summer went on and the heat came down hard, scum would rise and algae would take over.

Tonight, the water was clear, and as they topped the rise, the moon had just finished coming up over the far hills, big and heavy, full and bright, the pond reflecting the yellow glow with a clear shimmer.

When Zane's hand brushed hers, Waverley assumed it was an accident. But then it brushed hers again before his fingers wrapped around her hand and slid between hers.

"Is this okay?" He pulled her to a stop with their joined hands. She nodded, not trusting herself to speak.

He'd just told her he was spending time with her because he had to, and now he was holding her hand, and her heart wouldn't stop trying to fly away.

She found it hard to breathe, and she wanted him to pull her closer, while all the time she knew she was being a crazy, silly girl. A woman with six children of her own, and now four more, should know better.

"You know what I said earlier, or maybe what you said earlier, about me having to spend time with you?" he asked softly, his head turned down to her.

She nodded, trusting the full moon was bright enough for him to see. She didn't know what other answer he wanted her to give.

"It wasn't true. I mean, I know I need to spend time with you or that we need to do things together, things like this. But it's not a hardship for me to go in the house and work with you in the kitchen." His voice dropped. "I look forward to it. Not because I like kitchen work, but because I like working with you. Even better than working in the kitchen with you is when you come outside with me. I like seeing you in my world." He grunted. "I like seeing you drive my tractor." That last had a little smile in his voice, probably because they both knew she was a horrible tractor driver. She could drive a car decently, but there were a lot more knobs and levers in the tractor, and they scared her because she couldn't just lift up from the throttle and have it stop.

He tugged on her hand until she turned to face him. "After you leave, and I'm by myself again, I find myself wishing you were back. It's more fun to work when you're with me. It's scary, really, because I get spoiled. I like looking up and seeing your smile. I like sharing a joke with you. Liked seeing the wonder on your face when that fawn jumped out of the hayfield and ran down the fence row."

She hardly dared to breathe. He'd never said anything like that to her before, and if her heart beat fast before, it felt like it was about to explode now. She didn't want to move, she didn't want to break whatever spell had descended on him that had prompted him to say those things. She'd had no idea he enjoyed her company.

"Do you understand what I'm saying?"

She shook her head slowly. Maybe she did understand a little, but she wanted more. Needed more.

"I'm saying I know I need to spend time with you and that we need to do things together. But I do it because I want to, not because I have to."

She needed to swallow. Her throat felt stiff and scratchy, but her mouth was dry.

"I think this is where you tell me that you like my company too." There was a note of humor in Zane's voice, but also a touch of insecurity.

"I thought you knew that." Her voice was a breathy whisper. She wasn't sure how she even was speaking.

"I guess I can't read your mind any better than you can read mine."

She smiled a little at his words. They were so different. Him with his farm and all the things he'd built, and her just trying to survive, feeling like she'd been treading water forever and barely keeping from drowning. But inside, maybe they weren't that different. He wasn't any more secure than she was.

That might be something that she could help him with.

"So I think we've just agreed that we enjoy spending time together. Even if we just talk about the kids and their problems, and the farm and its problems, and problems in general." She meant to be kind of flippant and a little funny, but the words were too true to have much humor.

"Is it that bad?" He put a hand up, shaking his head. "Never mind. It is. We never talk about anything but problems." He looked off at the moon, huge and beautiful on the horizon and so close it felt like they could touch it. "Let's change that, right now." He barely stopped. "The moon's pretty." He couldn't say it without a smile, apparently, and a little chuckle. She joined him. She supposed if they were going to not talk about problems, it was going to have to be jarringly deliberate, like he'd just done.

"I think this is where you say something romantic about the moonlight in my eyes." She was being a little goofy, because he wasn't really a moonlight-in-the-eyes kind of guy. She was gratified when his teeth flashed.

"Could you give me an actual sentence? Because I'm having trouble coming up with something that sounds anything but ridiculously stupid in my head."

"Ridiculously stupid is okay. It's not problems anyway, right?"

"Okay, you asked for it...the moon is shining in your eyes; it looks like you have little bananas in them."

Waverley choked on a breath before it slobbered out. "I'm sorry. I just spit on you. I'm really sorry. But bananas? Yeah, you're right. Maybe I should help you." She cleared her throat. "You can say, 'Waverley, the moon makes your eyes look pretty.'"

"That's lame. It sounds like something a junior high kid would say." Zane waved a hand in the air, as though junior high was so long ago he couldn't be bothered.

"I'm sorry, but that was much better than the whole bananas thing."

"Can't argue with that. So, I guess we've come to the conclusion that if I had to actually court you before I could marry you, I might not have been successful."

"No. Bananas would have been funny, and funny is okay."

He smiled down at her, but his smile slowly faded as the silence dragged between them.

"I guess funny might be okay. But I feel more than funny when I'm with you."

The way he said it, it could have been taken as humorous, but she thought he was trying to be serious, and she wouldn't laugh at that. "I feel the same way."

She had thought she wouldn't give in to any little bone he threw her, but she didn't want to play hard to get. It just wasn't her style to play games with relationships and feelings.

She wanted to match his efforts with her own. Maybe they weren't exactly on equal footing, since she really liked him, and he had been more like stuck with her. But she wasn't going to sabotage any efforts that he made, any vulnerability he showed. That was just crazy. Plus, there was more going on under that confident exterior than she had thought to begin with.

Lots of new feelings and emotions ripped through her, maybe excitement and anticipation being the bigger ones. It was also noteworthy for what she didn't feel—neglected and isolated like she'd felt almost her entire first marriage. Maybe, just maybe, this would be different.

Zane's big hand squeezed hers gently. "Come on, let's walk down to the pond. The pond and your eyes are pretty with the moon shining on them." He gave her a cocky grin. "See? Quick learner, right?"

She had to laugh, and he shared the laughter with her. Together, it echoed across the night air and blended together. Similar in her thoughts to the way their hands twined together. Maybe their hearts and lives and kids would be the same, eventually.

# Chapter Fifteen

---

"Are you ready?" Zane asked.

The lunch dishes were done, and Waverley was setting some of her baked goods back on the counter.

Zane had helped her all morning with cooking and wrapping and knew the big order that someone in town was coming to pick up today was completely ready.

"I am. But I do need to be back here by 2:30. That's when Rachel said she was going to be here to pick this up."

"We'll be back in plenty of time. I have something I want to show you." He tried not to fidget. He was kind of excited about this and surprised he hadn't thought of it earlier. Well, he'd thought of it two weeks ago, but it had taken a little time for him to think about it and work on it so that it was good enough for him to show Waverley.

It had been hard, with planting in full swing, but he hoped it was worth it.

She smiled and walked out as he held the door for her, walking down the steps and slowing so he could catch up.

He took her hand, easy now and right. It would be strange to walk beside her and not hold it, after the weeks they'd spent taking walks after supper while the kids cleaned up the dishes and put the food away. A lot of times they weren't long, especially if any of the children had school projects that needed to be finished up before they read a book and sang, but they'd always managed to get at least ten minutes in.

He tried hard during those walks not to talk about problems, even if he wasn't very romantic.

There was a tenuous bond between them, and he'd like to see it become more, wanted it to be more, but he wasn't sure he was ready. Waverley wasn't Vicki, not in any way, but he still couldn't help but be a little concerned.

Afraid.

Trust was hard, even though Waverley had done nothing to not deserve it.

Her fingers tightened around his, and he looked over.

"Are we walking far?" she asked.

"I was gonna take the four-wheeler. It'll take less than five minutes to get there." He opened the door to the shed and followed her inside.

He got on first, so he didn't kick her, and she settled in behind him. Close. He liked that she didn't hesitate but put her arms around him and pressed against him.

That was trust, he supposed. It seemed to come easily to her, even though her first husband couldn't have been that much better than Vicki.

He supposed Dexter hadn't cheated. That made it easier.

But he hadn't taken care of Waverley the way she deserved, and yet there she was putting her arms around him and holding on, trusting him to keep her safe.

He bet she didn't even think about it.

"You've never ridden with me before. Aren't you afraid I'll be a bad driver?"

"I don't think I've ever seen you be bad at anything you've done. I'm guessing you grew up on one of these. But even if you didn't, I'm holding on, and if I have to, I'll shut my eyes. But I'm with you. And I'm sticking as long as you do."

There was a half-smile on his face, but he was looking at her and thinking, trying to process her words. It was kind of like what he thought. She trusted him, and he hadn't needed to show her that he could even drive.

She just trusted him. And yet, it was so hard for him to return that. Oh sure, he trusted her to drive him on the four-wheeler, he supposed, but he couldn't trust her long enough to tell her that he thought he was falling in love with her. That was so much harder. He didn't even know why.

He started the four-wheeler and backed out of the shed, turning and taking the field road that connected his two farms. He had to come out and cross the highway, and drive up along the side of it for half a mile, before he came to what he wanted to show her.

He stopped in the parking lot and shut the motor off.

He sat and looked at the building, wondering what Waverley saw. It was a little rundown.

One of the front windows was broken, although he had ordered glass for it, but there was plenty of parking area and plenty of counter space inside, and the previous owner had even left two display cases.

"There was a walk-in cooler inside, and in the last two weeks, I've had a repair man here, so it's running." He paused. Waverley didn't say anything, so he kept talking. "I have two keys in my pocket, and I was going to give you one. But I thought we could go in and walk around some, and you could tell me what you think."

"You're thinking of buying this?" she asked.

He supposed he'd started the story right in the middle, because he didn't know how to begin. "I told you I had bought a farm not long before we got married. This was on the farm, and used to be a restaurant, and then it used to be an ice-cream stand, and then they used it to sell produce. I've looked into zoning and licensing, and everything's ready if you want to get the ball rolling to get this inspected and have this for your baked goods. We can put ovens in, and there's already a cooler, and it wouldn't be hard to get it set up for you to base your business right here."

He let out a breath, unaccountably nervous. He'd been pretty sure that she was going to like it, but she hadn't moved behind him, her arms still wrapped around him, frozen almost.

He turned his head. The movement pulled her arms away, and she let them drop. He wished he'd stayed still. He missed them immediately. Moving, he pulled a leg over the four-wheeler and stood beside it.

"Do you want to go in?" Maybe his heart was in his throat. Maybe that's what the lump was.

She stood, swinging a leg over. "Of course."

He wasn't sure what to think. She seemed kind of happy. He supposed it was hard to picture Waverley jumping up and down and screaming in excitement, and that wasn't really what he expected, but he wasn't sure exactly what he had thought she'd do.

She walked toward the door, and he walked beside her, putting the key in the lock and opening it. Holding it for her as she walked in.

He'd swept and cleaned a little, not to his mother's standards, and probably not to Waverley's either, although she didn't seem to get upset over dirt and messes.

She wandered slowly through. It wasn't that large, and it didn't take that long. But she seemed to be smiling, and she drew her fingers along the counter and the display cases.

Cars went by outside, and he almost pointed out that she was set in a prime location, because anyone coming into or out of Cowboy Crossing would almost certainly go by, unless they took one of the back roads in.

He wanted to say they could order a sign, and come up with a name, and all the things that had been going around in his head since he'd come up with the idea, but from being the oldest of all the boys, he knew he had a tendency to push and direct rather than listen, and he really wanted to let Waverley take the lead.

But maybe it wasn't what she wanted.

She closed the door on the walk-in cooler, which was the last thing for her to see, and turned to him. "Thank you. This is amazing. Are you sure it's not going to cost too much money to get it fixed up?"

Maybe she was worried about the expenses. Maybe that's why she'd been so subdued. "I wouldn't have suggested it if I didn't have the funds to follow through. We can't do everything at once, and it probably won't be open at least until the middle of the summer, but we can start now."

He supposed she should be able to see the finances of the farm. Even if her name wasn't on the accounts. He'd keep that in mind.

"Oh. Okay."

"Are you just shocked? Or is there a problem?" He figured he might as well ask. "If you don't like it, we don't have to do it. I haven't sunk so much into it that I can't walk away. It's up to you."

Her eyes skittered around the floor until she turned to face him fully, a hand on the counter beside her. "I like cooking in the kitchen in your house. I like being there for lunch and talking to you and Dwight and Buck when you come in to eat. I like to have you come in and help me. I like being able to leave and spend an afternoon with you. I like having the children all around me while I'm working in the afternoon when they get off the bus. I guess, I feel like if we do this, I'll be moving out of all of that, and it will be more of a business and less of a family thing. Does that make sense?"

He hadn't considered any of that. He'd only thought that she would be like every other woman that he'd ever been around, Vicki being the main one, who wanted their own thing. Wanted to have their own business and their own space and their own prestige and their own success.

"You're saying you'd rather be at home?"

Her lips flattened a little, and she looked around the building again. As he watched her, he could see excitement and interest in her eyes, but he could also tell that there was conflict there as well.

"Not exactly. Well, maybe." She smiled and looked at him. "Can I want both?"

He grunted. "You want it all?"

She lifted a brow and shrugged a shoulder. "I guess that's the rub. We can't have it all."

She looked around, again, and spoke. "I didn't realize you had this, and it's so kind of you to even think of me with this, and I'm grateful, more than I can say. And there is a huge part of me that wants to do this, that loves the idea of this challenge, loves the idea of having my own place and a space to work, and I can even see that maybe you would still be around some, and the kids could get dropped off here after school, and in the summer it could be a family thing. But," she turned her eyes to him, "I think I'd rather be a successful farmer's wife and a good mother to my children, all of them, and this would take my attention away from what I truly want. And I'm not saying that other women are wrong for wanting exactly what you're offering to give me, and it's a beautiful thing, for them. But I know, in the long run, my baking business is not going to matter to me in twenty years, not like my kids and...husband."

She said the last word rather softly, and her eyes had skittered away from his.

Maybe she was embarrassed, although he couldn't imagine about what. If she thought that he would be disappointed that she was going to put him above her business, she could get rid of that notion.

It was just foreign. The idea that she would care more about their relationship than she did about making herself successful...he wasn't sure what to say. He certainly didn't deserve that position in her life. Had done nothing to deserve it, and really could do nothing. It was a choice that she made, and he was honored by it.

"I love it though. And I'm just overwhelmed that you would've thought of me and that you would've done all of this and be willing to do more, just for me. I don't want you to be upset."

He put his hands on her shoulders, always surprised that she was not as sturdy as what she seemed when he touched her. "I will never be upset with your honesty. I would not ever want you to do something just because you thought I wanted you to. And honestly, I'm a little shocked and overwhelmed that you would choose basically service to your family over the opportunity to be a successful businesswoman. It's a mindset I don't know that I've ever encountered before. And I'm not sure what I did to deserve this devotion to your family, because it's my family too, so you're devoted to my family beyond your own success." He stopped and huffed out a breath. "I just happened to be in the wrong bathroom at the right time, or I wouldn't be standing here overwhelmed by the breadth and depth of what you're willing to give to others rather than keep for yourself."

She shook her head, kind of dismissing his praise. "I think the world sees it as a lack of ambition. And that's probably what it is. Don't make it into some big great thing when it's really not."

He tightened his hands on her shoulders and shook her just a little, willing her to look up and meet his gaze.

She did.

"It is something big. It's big to me. Please don't minimize it."

For weeks now, he'd felt a growing attraction, a desire to be with her, to be closer, to touch her. But standing here having her reject what he'd been so excited about giving her should have upset him. Instead, it made his chest swell, and his heart grew big with feelings he could hardly contain.

His thumbs traced over her collarbone, and he studied the angle of her bone through her shirt.

He cleared his throat. "I've been thinking about something for a while now, but I'm just not sure how you feel, and that's important to me before I do what I want."

He'd just successfully managed to say nothing. Felt like he was about thirteen. With one failed marriage under his belt, and four kids, he should be able to do a little better job at what he was trying to get at.

But she flustered him.

He found he cared way more than he wanted to, which scared

him, but it had also come to the point that he wanted to move past the fear.

"I don't think I understand what you're saying." Her hand, which had been resting on the counter, landed lightly on his arm, her fingertips touching his wrist, moving down his forearm.

That touch drove all the words out of his mind and brain, and he couldn't remember what it was he'd wanted to say to begin with.

He hadn't forgotten what he wanted to do, though.

"I want to kiss you."

Her hand stopped.

His breath froze. Waiting.

The pulse in her neck skittered and flapped.

She took a half of a step closer and lifted her head. "Then what are you waiting for?"

His eyes flew to hers, which had deepened into a dark green-gray and held some of that admiration that he had craved since it had disappeared six weeks ago.

"I love it when you look at me like that."

Her mouth curved just a little, and her lips barely moved as she said, "Like what?"

"Like you think I could do anything. And you admire me for it." His head moved back and forth a little, although he hadn't intended for it to. "I can't do anything, and I don't deserve it, but man, I love the look."

Her touch made his arm burn, and he wanted to be closer, but he didn't want to ruin whatever it was that had been growing between them.

Not the attraction, although that had been growing, but the bond of friendship that felt delicate, like a spider's web, not strong enough yet to withstand anything hard. Still strengthening, and growing, every time they were together. If he kissed her right now, as much as he longed for it, it could ruin everything.

She'd asked him what he was waiting for, and he didn't know.

He didn't think the time was quite right. But he couldn't resist running a thumb along her jaw before he stepped back.

"Do you have Saturday afternoon free?" he asked.

Her face shifted, and he watched her sort through the different feelings as she adjusted to his abrupt subject change. He thought he saw disappointment fly across and maybe a little longing. Or maybe he just wanted to see that, because that's what he felt.

Still, after a few seconds, she was composed again, and her brow crinkled.

"Yes. I believe so."

"Good. Keep it free. The boys and I are working on something, and I think we can have a little bit of family fun if the weather cooperates."

"You mean Sunday afternoon?"

"No. Saturday. We'll still do something Sunday as a family too, but I wanted to take a little extra time this weekend. The planting should be almost done, and I should have most of the spraying finished as well."

"Okay. I'll try to make sure the kids have their schoolwork in good shape. We'll work extra hard Friday night."

He almost ended the conversation there. But he seemed to be addicted to touching her, and his hand went back up. His mouth opened at the same time with words that he hadn't thought about. But found to be true.

"I told you I wanted to kiss you, and that's true. Not today, but soon. Do you have any problems with that?"

He was nervous over that last question, because he was almost certain he knew the answer. Almost certain she wanted him to kiss her as much as he wanted to do it himself.

Sure enough, she had a confused look on her face as her head shook back and forth. "You never told me what you're waiting for."

"The right time. I want our first kiss to be the right time. After all, our timing has been pretty good so far, right? I mean come on, what are the odds of us being in that bathroom together? We don't want to ruin our timing streak."

"I think now is a really good time."

Maybe she'd just shown her whole hand to him, and he liked that. Liked that she wasn't afraid to let him know that she wanted more. It took a certain amount of trust on her part, and trust wasn't something he took lightly.

"Soon." He wasn't really a winking kinda guy, but he found that his eyelid dropped before he grabbed her hand and they turned and walked out.

# Chapter Sixteen

averley hung her sweater up on the hook and looked around the clean kitchen. The kids had done an excellent job of cleaning up. There might be a few crumbs under the table they'd missed. But not bad.

"You ready?" Zane asked as he walked in from hanging up his hat and taking off his boots. They'd just gotten in from their walk, and it sounded like the kids were all waiting for them in the living room.

Zane had been looking at her differently, although she couldn't exactly explain how. Except he was doing it again. Almost an intense look. One that said he *saw* her.

She wasn't sure if anyone ever looked at her like that before. She'd certainly never noticed. Every time she saw that look on his face, she shivered.

It was almost sensual. She wasn't used to that.

"I am." She walked to the doorway, and he met her there, slowing so she could pass in front of him. He put his hand on the small of her back, just a light touch, but it was the kind of touch her whole body focused on—where his fingers pressed into her skin, along with his presence behind her, the sound of his breath, the pad of his steps.

She couldn't believe she paid attention to all of those things. She hadn't even known someone's nerve endings could be that sensitive. She picked up a scent, stronger, the same strength and spice and dependability that he always smelled like.

As they walked into the room, John was already tuning her guitar. The kids usually had it out and ready for her, eager to do the family thing. It hadn't gotten old for them even after the almost two months they'd been married.

She hoped it never did.

Not for her, either. Zane had gotten into the spirit of things, and she no longer had the burden of both the story and the singing.

Most of the time, he read to them first, and sometimes, he told them a story of something he and his brothers had done when they were younger.

She didn't have any such interesting stories. All she remembered doing when she was a kid was sitting around the house waiting to go to school, learning to play her guitar, and cooking for her parents. She had a few nice memories of her grandparents before they passed away. And some memories of her brothers that weren't horrible but weren't great either.

John handed her the guitar, and she went and sat in what had become "her" seat in the corner. A couple of kids sat on both sides of her chair, and Zane always sat at her feet.

It surprised her at first, since he hadn't sat there the first week they'd been married.

She kind of thought after a hard day working outside, he would have appreciated the recliner or even commandeered the couch, but he did neither.

She'd been a little disconcerted at first with him at her feet, but she'd quickly grown used to it and now looked forward to it.

He settled down on the floor, legs stretched out in front of him and crossed at the ankles, with the book that they'd been reading opened to the chapter where they'd left off. The children sat down, several of the little ones getting their coloring out, and her older boys sprawled on the floor close to Zane, looking at him with almost hero worship.

Waverley looked around the room, though, since the girls seemed to be excited about something, whispering among themselves and huddling together beside the brown recliner.

If Zane noticed them, he ignored them. He lowered his head and cleared his throat.

"Daddy? Aren't you gonna tell us how it went? What did she say?"

Oh. Now Waverley could see what was going on. They had been a little quieter at supper and had looked at Zane in expectation. But Waverley hadn't given it much thought because she'd been deep in thought herself over what had happened earlier at the old fruit market.

Hoping that Zane wasn't upset that things hadn't worked out the way he'd been expecting.

He seemed okay, even happy, maybe, that she wanted to be home with her children and to focus on being a wife and mother.

But he must have told the girls, or all the kids, what he'd been going to do, although the boys didn't seem nearly as interested, and they wanted to know.

Zane read the chapter number, but when he paused to take a breath, she said, "Wait, please."

His chin jerked up. He looked over his shoulder with questions in his eyes. "What's the matter?" he asked, like he hadn't heard his daughters ask him to tell them how things went today.

She shook her head and looked over at the group of girls. Even Ophelia had a look of anticipation on her face. They'd all enjoyed helping her in the kitchen. She'd enjoyed it, too. They'd had fun. But she hadn't realized that maybe a bakeshop was something that they wanted. She had said no for herself, but maybe the girls were interested in making this a family thing for everyone.

She hadn't considered that.

"Are you girls talking about the bakeshop?" she asked, a little hesitantly because she could be way off base.

"I wasn't gonna talk about that. You made your decision, and I'm with you." Lines appeared between Zane's brows, and his look was assessing, like he was wondering why she was even discussing it.

She understood. She didn't want the kids to get all upset, and she appreciated him maybe trying to spare her from their anger, since if they were looking forward to it, and she was the one who said no, she was the one they were gonna be upset with.

She shook her head a little at him and then looked over to the girls. "This is something you guys were looking forward to?"

Four sets of heads nodded up and down, with Beatrice's pigtails bouncing and swaying.

"Why?"

"We like baking. We think it's fun," Ophelia said.

Tempted to say there was a lot more to baking than just baking, Waverley held her tongue. When the girls had helped her, she hadn't just allowed them to do the fun part.

"Everyone likes it when I bring goodies in to school. And my teacher's happy when I bring a healthy snack. No one else's moms send stuff in." This was from Juliet, and Waverley could hardly meet her big, blinking blue eyes. She looked so adorable with her long lashes framing them, sitting on her knees with her hands folded in her lap, bouncing up and down, like she was waiting for Waverley to announce that they would be opening a restaurant tomorrow. And that Juliet would be the head chef.

"Even if we don't do a bakeshop, I'll still send things in for your class," Waverley said, just in case there was some confusion as to whether or not she was going to be baking even if they didn't have the bakeshop. It could be something she did on the side when she had time. But not something that took over her life.

"I want to learn. And Daddy said if we had our own shop, then maybe I could help. And someday, maybe I could be a cook."

"I was looking forward to it, too," Cordelia said. Her lips were puckered though, like she could tell that there was something going on. That things weren't quite what they had been hoping and expecting.

"You want to, too?" Waverley asked Cordelia.

Cordelia was at that age where her friends were starting to be more important than her family. She hadn't shown that at home, since she'd lost the attitude within the first week that Waverley had been there. But Waverley was expecting the shift from wanting to be with her family to wanting to be with her friends.

"Yes!" She looked as excited as Ophelia. "You know I help you every chance I can. Some of my friends have been asking if they could come out and learn too. They think it's really cool that everything in my lunch is homemade. Especially if I've made it myself."

Zane had sat at her feet, not moving, and Waverley had been so focused on the girls and what they were saying that she almost shot out of her chair when she felt a touch on her foot. She bit back a squeal as she realized it was his rough hands moving over it.

She held her breath and forgot all about baking for about fifteen seconds while his hand went up and down over the top of her foot and wrapped around her ankle before going up and down again.

That was new.

That was *very* new.

She liked it. Except it made it really hard to concentrate on anything else.

Tempted to run her fingers over the top of his head and touch the skin of his neck, she resisted and tried to bring her mind back to what they were talking about.

Also, maybe his touch was meant to distract her and not to be as sensuous as it felt...maybe more of a hint. Although what he could be hinting for her to say, she wasn't sure.

She gathered her thoughts and tried to focus back on the girls. "When your dad and I were over there today, I told him that I wasn't interested in it, because it would take me away from the house, and from him, and from all of you. But…" she tapped her fingers on her guitar, "if this is something that you guys want, we'll be doing this as a family. If it's not just me, I'm definitely willing to get on board. In fact, I'm kind of excited about it."

The kids were young, and they might grow out of it, and of course she would be doing most of the work for the foreseeable future.

Cordelia was a huge help. So was Juliet. They both learned quickly, and both had spent every spare second they could with her. She would have plenty of help.

But she also knew that she probably shouldn't start a business based on the eagerness of young girls.

"I guess we can call this a family meeting, then," Zane said. "You girls can have a say in that, but then you need to realize, if you're gonna vote to do this, that's a vote for you guys all working on it too. This isn't gonna be something that Waverley does on her own. She wasn't interested in it on her own, but she sounds kind of excited about it, if it's gonna be a family thing."

Was that pride in his voice? She almost thought it was, but she couldn't be quite sure. His hand hooked around her ankle, and his thumb moved up and down over her shinbone, sending sparks up her leg.

She hadn't wanted to be away from the girls, but she hadn't wanted to be away from him either.

His chin jerked at the boys on the floor. "You guys have a say in this as well. If it's gonna be a family thing, it's gonna be a family thing. It's not good to be girls at the bakeshop and boys at the farm." He lifted a brow at them. "I think Waverley had the right idea. We can't be a family if we're split in all different directions. That means we'll still be doing farmwork, of course, because right now, that's paying bills. But it's gonna be us taking more work on because when we're done with that, we're gonna be going and helping them."

Matthew didn't look too interested, but Mark shrugged his shoulders. "We've been helping Mom make things since we were old enough to sit on the counter and crack eggs. That's not anything new for us."

Zane lifted his shoulder. "It might not be anything new, but are you willing to do it?"

"We'll still get to help outside with you?"

Zane nodded. "I'm counting on it. I was just talking to the man who owns the farm south of us about leasing some ground today. I haven't even gotten a chance to talk to your mother about it, but that will be taking on more work. And I'm expecting you boys to be helping me. I wouldn't have done it otherwise. But I'm saying I don't want us to be living a life somewhere and never see your sisters and your mom. We need to figure out a way to make it work so we're all doing this together."

His hand squeezed her ankle as the boys, the four oldest ones anyway, got very serious expressions on their faces.

Waverley couldn't see Ax nor Roman, because they were sitting on either side of her.

She held the guitar in one hand and reached down and stroked Roman's head. He put his hand up and patted hers. She figured that meant he was okay.

Maybe they were crazy for asking their kids for input. People would probably call them completely nuts. After all, only one was even a teenager. They were too young to know what they really wanted or to be able to truly consider the amount of work they were talking about.

Although this was probably something they would remember for their whole lives. That their parents asked permission. That they had a family meeting. That they were asked to give their input. That their parents wanted them to be involved. That they were waiting on their answers.

She supposed there wasn't too much that would make kids feel more a part of the family than to be involved in the decisions and then to be involved in the work that it took to support that family. She was pretty impressed with Zane's ingenuity.

The next time they went for a walk, she'd have to tell him that he'd taken to this father thing pretty naturally. At least in her opinion.

"Well, Dad, I'd rather be out in the field working. But it's not really fair for me to get what I want and they don't. If the girls want to have a bakeshop, and the only way they can do it is if I'm willing to give up a little bit for them, I will." Matthew's voice hadn't quite deepened into that of a man's, but he didn't sound like a little kid anymore either and had the occasional squeaks to show the change.

Still, it didn't need to have the timber of a man's voice in order for him to sound like a man. Which he did.

That was partly because he'd been forced to grow up early, because after Dexter died, Waverley had depended on his help to make things work.

She couldn't find it in her heart to be sad about that, though. She didn't think it hurt for kids to have responsibility and to grow up. Maybe, if things hadn't been as hard as what they were, he would still act like a little boy when he really didn't need to.

He seemed comfortable in his skin and proud that his opinion was being considered.

He'd been looking at Zane, but his eyes slipped to hers, and she smiled. She was proud of him.

"I agree," Mark said. Mark had a mind of his own, but unless he felt Matthew's way was completely wrong, he usually went along with it.

"As long as I don't get stuck washing dishes all the time," Luke said, "I'm okay. But I really hate washing dishes."

"I think there will be plenty of things to do. I imagine doing dishes will be some of it. But you seemed to be pretty good at scrubbing the floor. I think I saw you doing that on Saturday night?" Zane said.

Luke sat a little straighter in his chair, proud that his dad had noticed, and commented on, what a good job he had been doing.

"Yes, sir, you did. Mom said I did a good job, too."

"I think she told me that as well. But I could see it for myself."

John, a little more serious than the other boys even though he was younger, seemed to be thinking pretty hard about it. "What if I say no?" he finally said as everyone stared at him.

Waverley bit back a smile. Maybe the power would go to his head. He was usually very serious but also kind. "If you say no, we're definitely gonna take that into consideration. We want everybody on board, not just most of us."

"Really? You would not do it if I said no?" John asked, his eyes fixed on Zane.

Zane breathed out through his nose, then turned around and looked to Waverley. "All or nothing?" he asked, as though it was her decision.

Maybe he was just working the system, because she thought she saw a twinkle in his eye.

She nodded. "Yes. All or nothing."

"Cool. I get to make the decision." John jumped up, his hands spread. "Ladies and gentlemen..." He paused, for dramatic effect, probably. "We are going to open a bakeshop." He spun around and shot his fist in the air.

The girls didn't need much to light their excitement, and they were jumping up and dancing around the room before John had landed on his feet again.

The other boys were slower to get up, and Matthew never did get off the floor, although he sat up.

"Is it really gonna be a bakeshop?"

"Like a store?"

"Did someone say it might be a restaurant?"

"How do you start a restaurant?"

"Where are we going to do it?"

"The other night when I took the girls for a ride before supper while you guys were washing up, I took them to an old restaurant that had been turned into a produce stand. I told them that maybe Waverley would be interested in turning it into a bakeshop. I hadn't gotten a chance to say anything to you boys yet. But I was going to. I'll show it to you. Probably not tonight, because it's getting late. But sometime."

"We had a secret that you didn't know about," Beatrice said in a singsong voice, looking at Matthew.

Matthew pretty much ignored her, but Zane turned his head. "That wasn't nice, Beatrice."

She hung her head and whispered, "I'm sorry."

Zane said, "The boys have a secret that you girls don't know about. They won't be telling it until Saturday."

Waverley's head snapped up. What in the world could it be? He'd mentioned about her having Saturday afternoon off and keeping it free for the family. It must have something to do with that. She could hardly wait to find out what surprise Zane had for them.

# Chapter Seventeen

Saturday morning, there was palpable excitement in the house. Kids skittered through their chores, and even Waverley got caught up in the anticipation.

The evening before, Zane had been late, and she hadn't held supper for him. They'd missed their walk, but he'd come in in time to sing with them before bed.

However, on Thursday evening, she'd asked him what was going on Saturday afternoon.

Zane smiled more now than he had when they were first married.

The moon was waning, but she could see Zane's teeth gleaming in the moonlight.

"If I told you, it wouldn't be a surprise, right?" His hand squeezed hers, and his thumb rubbed over the back of her hand.

She loved the smiling, the humor, the laughter together. There'd been more of that in their walks. True to his word, he'd tried not to talk about problems, and she went along with it. If there were issues to discuss, they usually did it in a low whisper at night after they'd put the kids to bed.

Sometimes they were the only ones up in the morning, although often Zane was already out when she came downstairs.

If he was working somewhere where he could stop, he came in for breakfast. But that wasn't a regular thing.

She wished it were because she enjoyed being around him. He added not only excitement and a buzz of attraction across the breakfast table but companionship and a sense of teamwork, and she just plain liked him.

She supposed when a person liked someone, they enjoyed being around them and wanted to spend as much time with them as they could.

That was probably normal, as was her longing to do more with her husband.

Over the breakfast table, he talked some about how he'd set in motion some of the things he needed to do before they could open a bakeshop. State inspections and different construction issues that needed to be addressed before it was brought up to code.

Several of the boys knew what was going on later, and they had cheeky grins while they ate.

Zane himself couldn't seem to keep his lips from turning up, and he met Waverley's gaze across the table several times as she raised her eyebrows at him and he just shook his head.

She loved that silent communication as well. Where they looked at each other and knew what they were thinking and it didn't matter how many kids or dogs or how much noise or fighting there was around them; they could talk without words.

It definitely made her feel like there was a bond forming between them.

"If it's okay with you, we'll eat at our regular time and then head out. It's just a short walk to where we're going. If you want to have some goodies and drinks packed, that would be great, too."

Matthew and Mark grinned even wider, and Mark tried to unobtrusively quiet Luke with a finger across the neck when he opened his mouth. Luke snapped his mouth shut without saying anything, but his eyes were glowing as well.

"You guys have us all excited; this had better be good," Waverley said to Zane as everyone got up from the breakfast table and he came over to her.

"Oh, it's going to be good." Then his eyes sobered some. "I don't think this is gonna ruin your day, but I heard from Vicki. I don't think I ever told you..." A dog barked, a kid yelped, and there was a prolonged thump that made them both turn their heads. Ax, Roman, and Ophelia were in a pile with Billy and Bambi, and tails and legs and noses were all twisted up together. No one seemed to be hurt seriously, but Zane took Waverley's elbow.

"Can we step outside for a minute?" There was a touch of irritation on his face and also a self-effacing grin. Like he could hardly believe that all of the kids and all of this chaos was his, but she got the feeling that most of the time he liked it.

They stepped out the front door onto the seldom-used front porch, and he closed it behind them.

Her stomach crackled like a bag of dried leaves.

He'd mentioned Vicki. She knew there was nothing between Zane and Vicki, but it still gave her a sense of unease. Maybe because there wasn't much between Zane and her.

"Sorry about this, but I just found out late last night—I was already in bed—and I didn't want to wake you. I also didn't want to send a message; I wanted to tell you face-to-face."

She nodded, trying not to bite her lip. He looked so serious, but he hadn't dropped her elbow, and he stood close. She didn't mind that at all. Nor did she mind the absent way his thumb rubbed over the skin just under the sleeve of her shirt. It sent those crazy shivers shooting through her body, and it also made it hard to concentrate on his words.

"Just before you and I got married, the judge on our custody case issued an emergency injunction for me to have custody after Vicki dropped the kids off in a deserted place outside of town not far from where she lives and drove away from them. She's had issues like this for years and controls it with medication. Apparently, she went off her meds."

His thumb stopped, like his mind was going to what might have happened to his girls. "Thankfully, the girls were okay, obviously. But the state took them, and that's how I was finally able to get custody." He let out a breath that seemed irritated. "She's gotten herself straightened out, according to what she said, and in the emergency injunction, I have to allow her to visit whenever she wants to, up to three times a week."

His thumb, which had stopped moving as he talked about his girls, started moving softly over her skin again. "That's what I heard yesterday—that she's flying in, and she wants to see the girls. Sunday. I told her after church she could come home with us." He looked down and shifted some, and she had the feeling that he wanted to apologize for not checking with her first, but he didn't. "I hope that's okay."

"Of course it is. The girls need to see their mom. If that's what suits, that's what suits."

The lines on his face eased, and he looked at her with something that seemed an awful lot like gratitude. "Thank you. I didn't know how you'd react to that. I appreciate you being good about it."

"This has to be about what's best for the girls. Not about what I want." She meant that. She didn't always feel that way, but she always knew that was the way to be.

"Thank you. It seems like every time I talk to you, I feel like there's no way I can be to you what you are to me. I appreciate it."

Her eyes twitched; she wasn't sure exactly what he was saying, but it sounded like a compliment.

His hand tightened on her arm, and he pulled in a deep breath.

"I...I love the way you look in the morning. With your cheeks rosy and fresh and your eyes bright. You're always smiling. I don't think I've ever seen you in a bad mood in the morning. And there's a lot of laughter in the house. I...I guess I just wanted to tell you."

He could take her breath so easily. Whisk it away and make her heart run after it.

His hand reached up and touched the fine hairs at her temple, pushing them back and running his fingers behind her ear and down her neck.

"I wanted to kiss you today. Planned on it. Tonight." His look was a little sheepish for an instant before it grew serious again. "I'm thinking maybe I don't want to wait. How do you feel about that?"

As commanding as he was, as bossy and determined, he'd shown her deference both times he talked about kissing her, and she appreciated it.

She didn't really trust her mouth, but she stepped closer, one hand going to his waist, which was hard and warm under her palm, and the other sliding across the stubble on his cheek and wrapping around his neck. Tugging a little.

Maybe it was the tugging that made him grin.

"That didn't sound like a no," he murmured.

"It wasn't," she whispered, surprised she was still capable of forming words. Her arms ached, and she wanted to be closer, pressed against him.

Maybe he wanted the same thing, because he closed the distance between them and wrapped his arms around her, pulling her against him and lowering his head.

His lips met hers, and she gasped in surprise. Even that small touch was so much different than what she'd experienced before.

He took advantage of her gasp and slanted his lips across hers, making the porch dip and sway and causing her to cling more tightly to him, trying to anchor and steady herself as her body melted into his and her brain shut down and she quit thinking, just feeling—the rough scrape of his stubble, the heat of his hands, the hardness of his chest, the crazy zinging nerve endings, and the chorus of every cell in her body wanting more.

Kissing Zane was beautiful and subliminally dangerous, but it wasn't all she wanted. She didn't want to let go, didn't want it to end, didn't want to have to come back to reality.

Maybe the sun was still shining when he lifted his head from hers and touched his lips to the corner of her mouth and then her cheek and the angle of her jaw.

"I think there was a good reason to have not done this just now."

"Why?" She could barely form the word.

"I have zero desire to go do any of the things I was planning on doing today. Can't even remember them to be honest. I just want to kiss you again."

"Me too. Do it."

His deep chuckle vibrated through her body and tickled her ear, curving around until she felt it clear to her toes. Warm and good and perfect.

"There's nothing I want to do more. But we both have work we need to do today."

Her shoulders drooped, and disappointment seemed to pull down everything that had been so buoyant and joyful just a moment before.

"But it can wait, can't it?" he asked. Maybe it sounded more like a growl before his lips covered hers again. This time, she wasn't shocked but expected it—all the crazy, wild waves and lights and sparks. Expected it and welcomed them, pushing in and kissing him back fiercely, unable to modulate her response to anything less.

Something furry bumped into them, not hard, but they were so wrapped up in each other it knocked them both off balance. Zane's arm tightened around her while he caught them against the house with his other.

As her eyes opened, she saw he looked every bit as dazed as she felt. It took a little time to realize it was the dog that had hit them—one of their dogs. Another one was jumping around, yapping at their feet, while four or five of their children had come around the house.

The kids stopped short when they saw Zane's arms wrapped around her and hers holding him tight.

Maybe, if Zane's arms hadn't been so unmovable, she would have jumped back. Maybe she should have, from the shocked expressions on Ax's and John's faces. Juliette was smiling, but Beatrice looked every bit as shocked as the boys.

Cordelia, coming around the corner, stopped short with wide eyes. Waverley couldn't name the expression that finally settled on her face, but she thought it was a positive one.

Matthew and Mark were both grinning.

"Way to go, Dad. It's about time you give Mom some attention."

Waverley opened her mouth to tell Matthew not to be so disrespectful, but Zane said, "Shove it, you little whippersnapper. These things can't be rushed."

As he spoke, a grin broke out over his mouth, and he looked down at her. He murmured, "Maybe I can give you some more 'attention' later...or was that you giving me attention?"

She didn't know, but her silly grin matched his, she was sure. "I have no idea what the answer to your question is, but I'm all about doing it later."

He laughed, and his hands moved up and down her back before he loosened them, dropping one but keeping the other around her shoulders and holding her close to him.

She was fine with that. She couldn't think of anywhere in the world she'd rather be.

The dogs found something to chase and disappeared around the house with Roman and Ax running after them.

"I guess I'd better stop giving your mom 'attention' and go try to remember what I had planned to do today. This morning. We have a bunch of stuff to get done before we can show everyone our surprise."

Luke yelled and shot a fist in the air. If possible, Matthew's and Mark's smiles grew bigger.

Zane gave the boys some jobs to do, and Waverley gave the girls instructions on how to get started in the kitchen.

Once the kids and dogs and chaos had gone, Zane turned back toward her. "You okay?"

She nodded.

He didn't take that as a surface answer but seemed to stare deep inside. "No, I mean really? It was never my plan to kiss you for the first time and then go running off. Sorry."

"I wouldn't give it up. Or change it."

He let out a breath and closed his eyes before pulling her to him. She lay her head on his chest, and he lay his cheek on top of her head.

"Why couldn't you just say, 'stay with me, Zane?' It's what I want to do."

"You have work you need to do." She smiled, loving that he admitted he'd rather be with her.

"I'm having a hard time finding any desire to care about that. I guess it would be pretty awful to spend the morning just hanging out on the porch holding my wife."

"Just holding me?" There was a definite smile in her voice, and she was sure he was smiling too.

"And giving her 'attention.'" His chest shook. "Isn't that what Matthew said?"

"As long as attention is code for kissing, I don't think it would be a wasted morning."

"I have to agree with that."

"But if we're going to take the afternoon off for your surprise, we probably better not be that irresponsible." Was it irresponsible? She didn't really feel like it was. She felt like it was necessary. But not today.

"You're probably right." His head lifted. "I'd like one last 'attention' before I go, but that would probably be too big of a distraction." He loosened his arms and put a hand on the doorknob. "I'm thinking we'll be in early for lunch, though."

She laughed as they walked in together.

# Chapter Eighteen

"Hey, bro, thought you were coming over to get these fenceposts."

Zane ran a hand over his head. He'd completely forgotten about the fenceposts. He shifted the phone from his right hand to his left after settling his hat back down on his head. "Sorry, Chandler. Forgot. We got into a bunch of stuff here, and we have plans this afternoon. Maybe I'll swing by Monday and grab them."

"Sure. We'll plan on that."

They chatted for another minute before hanging up.

Zane shoved his phone back in his pocket, still not quite used to the fact that his playboy little brother had gotten married and become a responsible farmer.

Zane and the boys had been using the skid loader to trim the trees around the lower hilly field, and he'd been waiting on the far side for Matthew to get back. John and Ax had taken a shovel and were working on getting a couple of big stones out. Zane didn't actually expect them to get them, but they had wanted to try, and it wouldn't hurt anything. So he'd told them to go ahead.

Typically, he didn't have too much time to stand around, but he'd been so preoccupied today he didn't have things organized very well.

He hadn't expected to kiss Waverley this morning.

He didn't regret it. Not a bit. But holy smokes, it was hard to think about anything else.

It was hard to want to do anything else, aside from find excuses to go back to the house, since that was where he really wanted to be.

That was new. He typically didn't have any trouble at all thinking about the work he wanted to do and the things he needed to get done and organizing it all in his head.

A half an hour with Waverley this morning had totally shifted his mindset.

He found that dangerous, because he'd been determined that he wasn't going to get that wrapped up in a woman again. Wasn't going to give anyone the power over him that she could affect not just his emotional well-being but his spiritual and physical well-being as well. He couldn't make a woman his life.

He wouldn't.

Once was enough. If he hadn't learned anything else from Vicki, he'd learned that.

Not that Waverley was anything like Vicki, but it was the general idea. He couldn't let himself get so wrapped up in her that he lost himself, because when she left, it would feel like a part of himself went with her.

Although it was a fight, because that was what he wanted right now. He supposed that was what was meant when two became one. He stopped thinking of himself and started thinking of them as a couple. Thought of her.

But when it all went south, that just made it extremely painful to get himself separated.

What he felt for Waverley was so much stronger than anything he'd felt for Vicki. It would only be that much more of a mess.

It seemed like it took forever, but finally the morning was over. He'd only gotten half of what he wanted to get done and what he'd planned on, but that wasn't entirely his fault or that of the kiss he couldn't stop thinking about.

The boys were excited about their surprise. He couldn't blame them. He was excited about it, too.

Although he was mature enough to know that Waverley, at least, and possibly Cordelia, might not think much of it.

It was kind of a boy thing. It could be fun if they let it.

He hoped they would.

Maybe he didn't know Waverley as well as he thought he did, but he thought she'd go with it. She was all about doing family things together, and she liked the singing and the reading. Surely a little bit of playing together would be fun too.

The boys walked in the kitchen, boisterous and excited, and he came in behind, excited but more subdued, his eyes going immediately to Waverley whose back was to him as she turned the stove off and moved some pans around.

She turned, and just like him, her eyes sought him out immediately.

That made him feel good.

Their gazes met over the chaos in the kitchen, at least two dogs running around with all ten of their children, and there was yelling and talking and a squabble somewhere. The table was getting set, and the boys helped carry food to it.

Zane barely heard it all. It felt like forever that Waverley stared at him across what seemed like a very wide expanse of the kitchen. And then, he decided he was going to do what he wanted to do, and if she didn't like it, she'd need to say so.

He barely even finished the thought when his feet started moving, one in front of another, across the kitchen, around the table, and around the corner of the bar, the quickest and most direct route to his wife. He didn't stop until he was beside her and had his arms around her, and he did what he'd been thinking about all morning, bending his head.

Maybe she'd been thinking about it too, because she stepped into his embrace easily. Her arms slid around him, and her head lifted with a smile, her eyes bright and full of that look that he'd been longing for since the day they got married.

It almost stopped him. He wanted to see it and enjoy it. But he wanted to kiss her more. So he didn't stop, lowering his head and pressing his lips to hers, which opened easily under his, and the noise of the kitchen faded away, and all the heat and fireworks he'd felt this morning came back in a rush that made his knees weak and his arms tremble.

"Hey, look, Dad's giving Mom attention again."

Zane wasn't sure which one of the smart-aleck boys had said that, but Waverley's lips smiled, and so did his. They broke apart just enough to look each other in the eye and share grins.

"That's your kid," he had to say.

"He acts like you." She looked happy about that too, which made his chest swell even bigger.

"I was thinking I want to move out of the spare room. Soon." He had been thinking that. True. But he hadn't been expecting to say it to her. Not yet.

But her eyes didn't cloud like he thought they might. Maybe he was going too fast. But he didn't think so, not from the look on her face. Her brow twitched, and her smile curved into something that made him think of Eve in the garden.

"I'd like that," she whispered softly.

Tonight. He wanted to move tonight. This morning, it hadn't even been on his list of things he was doing in the next month, and all the sudden, it was a priority.

"Are you guys gonna quit that, so we can eat? I want to show the girls our surprise." Luke came over and poked him in the hip with his pointer finger. "Daddy? You promised we'd eat quickly. This is not quickly."

"The kid's smart like his mom," Zane couldn't resist saying, not wanting to drop his arms and shift away from her. Not even to eat.

"He's demanding like his dad," Waverley returned, with one brow arched.

"I don't think you've seen demanding," he said.

Her eyes widened, and her brow shot up. "Should I be scared?" There was a little flirt in her tone, but he didn't miss the touch of anxiety that floated across her face. Maybe that was a subject he shouldn't joke about. Not yet.

"No. The last thing you need to be is scared." If he did move out of the spare room, and it probably wouldn't be tonight, fear wasn't the emotion he wanted his wife to feel.

So far, Waverley had surprised him. He'd thought of her as mousy and nondescript. But her eyes flashed, and her face was alive with expression, and she hadn't backed down from anything. It took a woman with a strong amount of determination and perseverance to look at four more kids and decide to become a mother to them all. She wasn't the kind of woman who got scared easily.

"I'll try to remember that."

"Do. Because I mean it. There are a lot of things I want you to feel, but fear isn't one of them."

The kids were clamoring, and they broke apart. Waverley looked around her, like she was trying to get her bearings. Kind of the way he was all morning at work. Just slightly off-kilter because he couldn't get her out of his mind. Maybe she felt the same.

Lunch couldn't go quickly enough, and eventually they all were traipsing out, wearing the clothes he'd suggested, much to Waverley's interested glances.

The boys led the way. They knew exactly where they were going, and they branched off the pond road and went west around the back of the barn and down into the dip.

As they came over the hill, the girls started pointing and trying to figure out what was at the bottom.

The kids were far enough ahead of them, along with the dogs, that Waverley looked at him and said, "That looks a little bit like a volleyball net, only it's lower than I would expect, and it looks like you put it up over a mud puddle." She said the last kind of uncertainly, like she knew it was true but hoped that it wasn't.

"You are right on all counts," he said.

She bit her lips, studying the net and the mud and the kids and turning to look at him. Their linked hands had been swinging between them, but her grip tightened.

"So, does this mean..." She slanted narrowed eyes at him. "Mud volleyball?"

"Guilty." His grin was guilty too.

She hadn't quite gotten to the happy anticipation that the children were all showing. He wasn't sure she ever would.

"Am I playing?" she asked with a note in her voice that made him think she was hoping she wouldn't be.

Zane wasn't sure what kind of look was on his face. But it made her eyes widen before she smiled, a little shyly maybe.

Getting dirty was something kids enjoyed, boys in particular, probably. Along with mud. It wasn't really something he was looking forward to.

What he *had* been looking forward to, even before he kissed his wife this morning, was being beside her.

The mud would just make it more interesting.

"I hope so," he finally said, although he didn't think the words were necessary. She could tell by the way he was looking at her exactly what he wanted.

"I'm seeing a side of you that is surprising me," she finally said in a shocked whisper.

"Surprise is okay. Disappointment, not so much."

Her lips pursed as she shook her head. "There is no disappointment. Maybe I should have said pleasantly and interestingly surprised."

Maybe his grin looked smug. It sure felt that way. He'd take pleasantly surprised.

He wasn't sure there were too many women in the world who would look at a volleyball net set up over a mud puddle, and know he was expecting them to step into it, and say they were pleasantly surprised at finding out their husband wanted them to do such a thing.

He'd definitely gotten a one of a kind.

Maybe his heart would be safe with her.

He wasn't sure where that came from, but he pushed the thought aside. He knew better. And he didn't want to think about it.

"I figured you and I would be on a team with the younger kids, and we'd play against the older ones." He'd been angling in his head how he could justify being on the same team as Waverley.

Because, he had to admit, he wasn't the slightest bit interested in playing mud volleyball if she wasn't beside him.

He was enough of a realist to admit that even if he was standing beside her, that might not be enough to make *her* interested in playing.

Obviously, she was going to.

"I'm glad you said that. Because the only way that I want to have anything to do with this is if I get to do it with you."

It was like she could read his mind. He loved that.

They divided the kids the way they said, and Billy, one of her dogs, the terrier mix, thought he was part of the kids' team, although he didn't quite understand the rules of the game and tried to eat the ball rather than hit it.

"We better get the ball out of his reach, or we'll end up not having one. We'll have to figure out a way to play mud baseball," Zane said as he toed his boots off.

Most of the kids already had their socks and shoes off. The weather had thankfully cooperated, and it was well into the eighties. Plenty warm.

Waverley plopped down beside him. "So this is why you wanted everyone to wear old clothes and why you told the girls how much you like their hair in braids."

"Busted." He gave her his little-boy grin, the one that had always melted his mother's heart.

He didn't think Waverley needed her heart melted. She wasn't looking at him sternly to begin with but with a lopsided smile on her face.

"Why didn't you say the same to me?" She waved her hand over her head. "I would have braided my hair too."

"Hand me the clip that's on your wrist, and I'll braid it for you. Face that way."

Maybe she didn't think he knew how to braid, because she looked at him oddly before she turned. He had his hands in it earlier, and it was softer than he thought it would be. It smelled amazing, too, like yeast and cinnamon and a mature woman smell that reminded him an awful lot of kissing and moonlight and tender smiles.

He breathed deeply the whole time as he divided her hair into three ropes and wove them back and forth, clipping them at the end. He ran his fingers down her neck and lightly across her back as he let the braid go.

"There you are. Done."

He wanted to stay where he was and maybe put his lips where his fingers had just been, but the kids were begging to start, and now wasn't the time for that.

It took a little while to figure things out, but eventually he was standing on one side of the net, ankle deep in mud, which after the first couple squishes actually felt good, and Waverley was beside him, her feet bare and mud squishing up between her toes as well.

She'd given him a grin, along with a disgusted face, at first, but as they took a few steps, she said, "This is actually pretty cool. I don't know if I've ever walked through mud before. Definitely not in my bare feet."

"It's fun. No doubt. And in case you're wondering, I just figured we'd all go sit down in the creek to rinse off when we're finished."

"I hadn't even gotten that far. Normally how to clean up the mess is the first thing I think of before I've even made one. Somebody has me distracted today." She gave him a look that singed his eyebrows and made him wish that the kids were in bed.

Beatrice, Ophelia, Ax, and Roman were all on their side, and the six older children were on the other side.

"I guess we better let you guys go first, since the adults are both over here." Zane tossed the ball to Matthew, who caught it with a snap of his wrist. He tossed it right back.

"Nah. You guys are old, and they're little. We're going to win. You guys go ahead and serve first."

"Old?" There had been a lot of times in his life where Zane had felt old. Funny how fighting with Vicki had done that to him.

But today? Today, he felt like a teenager again. Something about the way Waverley was looking at him, or maybe it was the way she'd kissed him. It had made him feel like there was a lot more life left to live.

He shoved the ball under his arm and squished through the mud to the net. "The only fair way to do this is rock paper scissors." He held his fist out, and Matthew met him at the net.

It ended up he won, doing scissors to Matthew's paper, so he handed the ball to Ophelia since she was the youngest. "We'll just let her toss the ball over, since she won't be able to serve." He shot a questioning look at Waverley who nodded, then looked over the net at the older kids.

"If you guys need special privileges, go ahead and take them," Matthew said with a smirk. "We'll win fair and square."

# Chapter Nineteen

Waverley held Opehlia's hand in one of hers and Roman's hand in the other as they walked toward the house. They'd been completely covered in mud when they were done with the volleyball game. Instead of trying to take everyone home to get cleaned up, they'd all just gone and sat down in the creek.

Now they were wet and cold since the sun had gone down. The little ones were shivering as the dogs plodded along, drenched, but clean, and completely tuckered out, too.

Waverley was cold on the outside, but she couldn't keep from smiling, and it was hard to take her eyes off her husband who walked ahead of her holding Ax's and Beatrice's hands, while listening to Matthew and Mark, who couldn't believe that Waverley's and Zane's team had beaten them.

Her body was freezing, but her heart burned in a good, cozy way. She hadn't known it was possible to be this happy.

They'd eaten the food they packed, but everyone was hungry, so as kids were getting cleaned up, she cooked hotdogs on the stove and made macaroni and cheese. Simple, but it would work for tonight.

Zane had gone out with the two older boys to check the stock and feed. Once supper was over, they didn't take their normal after-supper walk, but got cleaned up instead.

The kids were blissfully tired, and since it was such a nice evening, they sat out on the porch to sing, Waverley with her guitar, and two little ones on either side of her.

When they sang inside, Zane sat at her feet. She almost liked being outside better, because he stood against the railing on the other side of the porch, opposite from her, leaning against the post and staring at her.

It was a look that made her insides melt.

She couldn't meet his eyes or she stumbled over the words, but she had a hard time getting her gaze to want to go anywhere but him. Even if he weren't good to look at, he was good to think about. The way he'd taken her kids and treated them as his own, the way he'd made time for them as a family, and her as his wife, the way he'd been looking for ways to do better, to correct anything that he'd done wrong in his first marriage, and she believed it wasn't just because he had to.

She'd gone from picking up her cross every day and carrying it because she had to in her first marriage, to feeling loved and admired and respected, especially when Zane looked at her in that certain way he did. The way he was right now.

She had no idea what her face showed, but she definitely returned those feelings, and couldn't help but feel she'd gotten a blessing far beyond anything she ever thought she'd have with a capable, hard-working man who seemed to put her wants and needs above his own.

She only hoped she did the same for him.

They put the children to bed as they normally did, each of them checking on the different rooms separately.

Zane almost always finished first, and usually she didn't see him again until morning.

But tonight, he was waiting for her, or seemed to be, standing outside the spare room where he slept, leaning against the doorjamb as she closed the door to the girls' room.

Her stomach contracted, not quite painfully, and her heart sped up.

She had no breath. Then too much.

She dug her fingernails into her palms and made her feet go one in front of the other toward her husband, even though she was tempted to turn and hurry into her room.

Which was actually his.

That wasn't what she wanted, not truly, but she wasn't sure she had the confidence to go after what she really wanted.

Another footstep. Closer.

And another.

The pain in her palms kept her grounded, and somehow she got enough breath to keep the dizziness at bay.

She stopped in front of him, closer than arm's length, and near enough to smell the strength and honor that his scent always reminded her of.

Her throat was too dry to even think about swallowing, and she took a deep breath through her nose, relaxing into it, before she opened her eyes and lifted her head.

He hadn't said anything. Hadn't moved.

She could be wrong, but she figured he was probably waiting on her. He'd told her earlier what he wanted, and she agreed, but he was probably still allowing her to choose.

She'd never had to say anything of the kind before, never had to be the one to issue the invitation.

She flexed her fingers, and then balled them into a fist again, digging right back into her palms.

He still didn't say anything.

She bit her lip, trembling. Walking over had taken courage, but opening her mouth was proving to be even harder.

Why? She was almost certain this was what he wanted too. He

wouldn't be standing there if he didn't. His 'yes' was almost a guarantee.

Still, the words wouldn't come. She stood in front of him, struggling to breathe.

Maybe it was the coward's way out, but she didn't have to start out with an invitation.

"I had a good time today." Her words were scratchy and her voice odd.

Seconds ticked by. He remained still and silent.

"Thank you for taking the time to play with us." She tried again. The scratch was still there, but her words were slightly more confident.

Still, he didn't move, and didn't talk.

She took a trembling breath, and said, "I liked singing outside."

She pulled both lips into her mouth when he remained silent.

Why wasn't he saying anything? Why was he just standing there? Maybe she didn't understand. Maybe there was something she'd missed.

And then she remembered.

He seemed so strong. So confident. Arrogant even. Sure of himself and capable.

She looked to him for support and guidance, as the children did, and he hadn't let any of them down.

But she remembered what she'd thought weeks ago. The impression she'd gotten, and what she'd caught glimpses of.

Vicki's rejection had stung. More than stung. It had scarred him. Invisibly, but she'd thought that while he still might be confident in all the areas she could see, emotionally he'd been crippled, and was completely insecure.

She could be wrong. She'd been wrong about so many things. But she knew how she felt, and telling him might not make any difference, but it didn't hurt her to be vulnerable, after everything he'd done for her.

She leaned closer, wanting to speak softly. It was easier.

"I love you. I just wanted you to know that."

He tensed, but still seemed to be waiting.

Swallowing, she said, "I admired you today, and every day since we've been married. Your work ethic, what you're doing with the children...and what you've done for me. I'm not a little girl that changes with the wind, and I'm not naive that I don't see any faults. But I wanted you to know, what I feel for you isn't just about the attraction that I feel, but it's about who you are. I love it all. That's not going to change."

He hadn't moved, but the air around them had become charged, and his chest moved up and down, faster and deeper.

"I don't have much," she continued, "but everything I have is yours."

She put her hands on his shoulders and slid them around his back, stepping closer and pressing into him. Her voice lowered. "I was hoping you might move into my room tonight?"

She wanted that to come out with confidence, but it ended up being a question.

He never did say anything, other than maybe a soft growl as he lowered his head to kiss her.

It was a long time later as she lay snuggled against his side, her arm thrown over his chest and his arm holding her tight, his fingers moving up and down her ribs, that he turned his head toward her, his nose pushing into the hair above her ear. In a voice, whisper-soft and rough, he said, "I love you too."

# Chapter Twenty

Sunday morning meant chores and church, but Zane had lain in bed and watched the sun come up over the mountains in the distance over the shoulder of his wife, as her body lay spooned with his, her head on his arm, her hair in his hand, and their legs tangled together.

He wasn't sure he actually could get out of bed, but he knew he didn't want to.

First morning since he could remember the sun had beaten him up.

He wasn't too worried about the animals, since he'd told Matthew and Mark last night when he said good night to them, that he'd let them handle the stock in the morning.

They were good for it.

And he'd been hoping...

He hadn't been sure, but he had definitely been hoping.

Waverley hadn't let him down.

It was a new feeling, being with a woman who didn't let him down.

Being with a woman who looked at him like he was more than he ever thought he could be, and who acted like she not only loved being with him, but loved doing anything that would make him happy.

It had made him want to do the same for her.

He was a little ashamed that he hadn't started it. She shouldn't have had to take the lead and shown him that she would be happy with him, serving him.

Wasn't that the Christian life? Service to others?

It began at home. She'd shown him that.

Which in turn, had made him search for ways that he could do the same for her. He'd thought of the banjo that he'd bought and hidden behind the couch, the store that he was slowly fixing up and the improvements he had planned for her kitchen here.

All things he wanted to do for her – because he was constantly searching out things he could do that would make her smile.

In the process, he'd fallen in love.

Sure, all the good attraction feelings were there, but there was a deeper, stronger feeling that wasn't about attraction, or anything physical, and was all about the person that she was, and the man she made him.

Not only that, because of their evening walks, because of how easy she was to talk to, she'd become a friend.

It was a new idea, thinking of his wife as his friend.

His best friend. He liked the thought and couldn't think of anyone he'd rather be with.

Of course, he couldn't sleep in every morning, but a man could have at least one morning as a honeymoon, right?

He kinda figured Matthew and Mark would make it so that he could have more.

Although, he also hoped the lady would enjoy waking up in her husband's arms. Because if she didn't, his happiness would fade.

He got a feeling he was about to find out, as she moved, and stretched. Turning a bit, but not opening her eyes, a small grin on her face and a satisfied look.

He didn't want to wake her, but he couldn't stop from touching his lips to her forehead.

Her eyes opened, slowly. Her smile grew bigger. He couldn't not smile back.

They probably looked ridiculous, exchanging silly grins. Then she moved.

He froze, before he did too, and then it was a long time before he thought about silly grins, or waking up, but there was no doubt in his mind that his wife was glad to wake up in his arms.

———

Waverley hummed under her breath as she moved around the kitchen.

Still pleasantly happy and content, trying not to look at the clock to figure out how many hours until bedtime.

Her cheeks had probably been fire engine red the whole way through the church service. Not from any particular embarrassment, necessarily. More from excitement and anticipation. Which shot all through her veins every time her husband looked at her.

Maybe she was glowing. She sure felt like it.

Even Vicki, sitting in the living room with their girls, hadn't dampened her spirits at all. Far from it. Although she did feel a little sad for Vicki, who looked tired and wan and couldn't seem to dredge up a smile, even though her girls ran to her calling "mommy, mommy!" which would have been enough to make Waverley split her face grinning.

Zane had gone out to the barn with the boys, kissing her tenderly before he did, and asking in a whisper if she was okay.

She smiled and nodded, confident that there was nothing for her to be worried about.

Now, when the outside door opened, she assumed it was him coming back, and she chopped the last few peppers, that same excitement bunching and tightening her insides. It still felt like forever until bedtime, but she wouldn't mind spending a few hours just looking at her husband. Or maybe he was coming to help with supper. Or coming in to take her for a walk. Or maybe he needed help. Whatever, she was looking forward to it.

But it wasn't her husband's head that poked in when the door opened.

It was John, followed by Mr. Freely, the Hollywood director.

Waverley couldn't keep her brows from shooting up. "Mr. Freely. I wasn't expecting you today. I hope you're not here to pick any orders up. I don't usually make things on Sunday. Did I miss something?" She tried to think, but she was almost positive she hadn't missed an order.

He held up a hand. "Relax," he said. "I just happen to be in the area again, with a little business I had to do with Loyal and Madeline. Although I've had a hard time getting your sweet rolls out of my head. Is it okay if I come in?" He stepped into the kitchen.

"I'm sorry. Of course. Come on in. I'll get some coffeecake out and cut you a piece. Unless you want something healthier. I was making a salad." She wasn't exactly flustered, but her mind had been so far from anything having to do with Mr. Freely.

Mr. Freely's eyes scanned over the counter, taking in the corn and beans and peppers that she had out. He pulled out a chair and sat down at the table.

"That looks like some kind of Southwest salad. I think I'll try it if you don't mind."

"I don't mind at all."

As she got a bowl begin to prepare a salad, he said, "Not too much. I don't have a lot of time. Just a taste."

"Okay." She did the calculations in her head as she added ingredients to his bowl.

"I've been thinking a lot about you here in this little town in Missouri."

She glanced over her shoulder as he put his elbows on the table and steepled his fingers.

"I'm pretty confident that there would be open doors for you if you wanted more out of your life than just this town, and what you have here." His pause seemed deliberate, but Waverley didn't turn. "I heard rumors in Cowboy Crossing that maybe you got married because you had to, and not because you wanted to. I can't offer you a big break, but I can offer you a paying position that would put you to good use doing something that, I think, you love."

Waverley listened as she put his salad together. She didn't put much in the bowl, because the more he talked, the less she wanted to hear. She doubted he wanted to hear her response.

She turned, and saw that John hadn't left, but was standing at the doorway, his eyes on the man, then his eyes went to her as she carried the bowl to the table.

They were big, and a little scared looking, and she wanted to reassure him, but he looked at her hand and the bowl she was holding, then back at the man, then ran out the door before she could open her mouth.

John was always so serious, and he had a tendency to take things with deep contemplation, odd for such a young child. She'd have to make sure she said something to him later.

"Here's your salad." She sat it in front of him, but she didn't sit down, walking around the table and standing behind a chair. It wasn't the most polite thing she'd ever done, but she didn't want to give him any false ideas about her interest.

"Would you like a drink?" she asked, not wanting to be rude.

He nodded, his mouth already full. Grabbing a glass and some ice, she filled it from the tap.

In her most pleasant voice, she said, "I can see how you'd maybe get that idea. And I understand, the rumors in town. They're mostly true."

He interrupted her. "This dressing is amazing. I can taste vinegar, I think. But there's some kind of spice you have in it that I don't recognize."

Although she wanted to be clear about her position, she talked to him a little bit about the dressing. It was a recipe she'd made up herself, one the kids enjoyed, and one that helped them eat the vegetables she served. She hadn't thought of it as anything special. In fact, she called it her "kid" dressing. It definitely wasn't her favorite.

"And you came up with this on your own?"

"Yes."

"Amazing." He put another bite in his mouth. His bowl was almost empty.

She moved back to the counter, continuing with her meal preparations.

After chewing and swallowing, he said, "Do please consider what I offered. I am almost one hundred percent sure that with recipes like this we can break into the industry. Especially considering the people that you know. Namely Chandler Hudson, and Madalyn."

Waverley had her back to him, as she stood at the counter getting the rest of the ingredients together to make a bigger salad for supper for her family. She finally turned, because she didn't want to have her back to him while she was turning him down.

Zane stood in the doorway.

Her heart skipped a beat, then thudded. His eyes were hooded. He didn't smile, didn't return her smile.

Maybe he'd heard Mr. Freely's offer. Maybe it had reminded him of Vicki being tempted by bigger and better things and he was worried she'd changed her mind about them and didn't love him anymore.

Maybe he decided he didn't love her after all.

She scoffed at that last idea and shoved it out of her brain.

Zane wasn't the kind of man who wavered to and fro depending on what was happening around him.

He was steadfast and sure. He'd whispered last night that he loved her. It wasn't something that was going to change this morning no matter what she did.

But he didn't need to worry. She didn't change that easily, either.

Giving her husband a wide smile, she said to Mr. Freely, "No thank you. I appreciate your offer, and it's very generous and very kind of you to think of me. You're still welcome to come back and order baked goods if you'd like, of course. My daughters and I are going to go into business together. I'm sure you'll hear about it when you come back. But I'm not going anywhere. I'm happier than I ever thought I could be, right here."

Zane hadn't taken his boots off, but she didn't care, as he walked across the kitchen and around the table and took her in his arms, lifting her up and kissing her.

She dropped the knife before she put her arms around his neck and kissed him back.

# Epilogue

Reid Hudson walked out of the back room of Cowboy Crossing's feed store. The numbers for the unofficial Single Dad Support Group meeting had been dwindling.

No one had ever kept anyone who wasn't a single dad out, and his brothers still showed up occasionally, even though they'd been finding their happily ever afters. But, honestly, he was starting to feel, more and more, like he was missing out.

It was still warm for September, and the night breeze wasn't cold as it blew down the back alley and swished across his face.

He always loved this time of year. Harvest time. When the work of the summer was realized by cash in the bank or crops in the barn.

He wasn't feeling it this year.

What was the point? Really. With just him, and one of his twins, it was hard to see why he'd keep doing this year in and year out.

Especially with his brothers looking so happy and hurrying out of the meeting, if they even bothered to come.

He used to hurry home.

Even in high school, anything that kept him away from Emerson was something he'd hurry through, always wanting to be with her, spend time with her, talk to her.

The future had seemed so bright and exciting.

Even when they'd been expecting the twins, things had looked up.

But the complications and the medical bills had been more than they could handle, and when her dad had offered her a position in his expanding company, she'd left.

He'd expected her to come back.

She'd, apparently, expected him to go get her.

They'd settled on a six month schedule where she got one twin while he had the other, then they switched, and neither of them had been willing to apologize or try to make things right.

"Hey, Reid. Good to see you." Zane slapped him on the back as he hurried to his pickup.

Zane was the most annoying person at the meeting tonight, although Reid loved that his brother was happy. He hadn't been at a Single Dad meeting for six months and it was great that he'd gotten out. Still, it'd be nice if the man could stop smiling for at least a minute, maybe two.

Reid suspected the only reason Zane had even gone to the meeting was so he could announce that Waverley was expecting.

How the man could smile and joke about adding an eleventh child to their crazy zoo – and grinning about eventually making it an even dozen – Reid had no idea.

Their mother had told Reid a few months ago that Vicki, Zane's ex, had gotten remarried and had not been fighting about custody anymore.

That could be a source of Zane's happiness, too.

Reid wasn't sure, but just knew his serious, older brother hadn't smiled that much in a very long time, if ever.

Unfortunately, Reid wasn't interested in divorcing Emerson, even though he'd not seen her in eight years, and finding someone new.

Just wasn't.

But he also wasn't interested in swallowing his pride and trying to win back his wife.

Especially with the massive mistake he'd made with his farm.

Money issues had driven her away the first time. Unless he figured something out, what he went through last time would be tiny compared to what he was about to go through. He couldn't try to reconcile with his wife when he was about to go through the worse financial disaster of his life.

Shaking all that aside, he thought about Houston, his son, waiting at home. Maybe he'd still be awake and they could watch Houston's favorite movie – that one about the twins whose parents were separated and they managed to trick them into getting back together.

It was a nice thought and a good movie, and Reid figured Houston harbored a secret desire for his own parents to get back together. Eventually Houston would grow up and realize that nothing like that ever happened in real life.

———

Join Jessie's list and be the first to know about new releases and sales on her books!

Read My Dearest Emerson, previously titled *A Second Chance in the Show Me State*, the next book in the Cowboy Crossing series. Reid and Emerson are high school sweethearts who need a second chance. Keep reading for a sneak peek now.

# A Gift from Jessie

*View this code through your smart phone camera to be taken to a page where you can download a FREE ebook when you sign up to get updates from Jessie Gussman! Find out why people say, "Jessie's is the only newsletter I open and read" and "You make my day brighter.  Love, love, love reading your newsletters.  I don't know where you find time to write books.  You are so busy living life. A true blessing."  and "I know from now on that I can't be drinking my morning coffee while reading your newsletter – I laughed so hard I sprayed it out all over the table!"*

Claim your free book from Jessie!

# Escape to more faith-filled romance series by Jessie Gussman!

***The Complete Sweet Water, North Dakota Reading Order:***

*Series One: Sweet Water Ranch Western Cowboy Romance (11 book series)*

*Series Two: Coming Home to North Dakota (12 book series)*

*Series Three: Flyboys of Sweet Briar Ranch in North Dakota (13 book series)*

*Series Four: Sweet View Ranch Western Cowboy Romance (10 book series)*

***Spinoffs and More! Additional Series You'll Love:***

*Jessie's First Series: Sweet Haven Farm (4 book series)*

*Small-Town Romance: The Baxter Boys (5 book series)*

*Bad-Boy Sweet Romance: Richmond Rebels Sweet Romance (3 book series)*

*Sweet Water Spinoff: Cowboy Crossing (9 book series)*

*Small Town Romantic Comedy: Good Grief, Idaho (5 book series)*

*True Stories from Jessie's Farm: Stories from Jessie Gussman's Newsletter (3 book series)*

*Reader-Favorite! Sweet Beach Romance: Blueberry Beach (8 book series)*

*Blueberry Beach Spinoff: Strawberry Sands (10 book series)*

*From Strawberry Sands to: Raspberry Ridge (12 book series)*

***Swoonfully Jolly Holiday Stories:***

*Holiday Romance: Cowboy Mountain Christmas (6 book series)*

*Cowboy Mountain Christmas Spinoff: A Heartland Cowboy Christmas (9 book series)*

*New and Much Loved: Mistletoe Meadows (4 books and counting!)*

*Laughing Through the Snow: Christmas Tree, PA Sweet Romcoms (6 short reads)*